KHALID MOHAMED
during his teenage years for (
He then covered crime, politics and the arts for *The Times of India,* Mumbai, from the mid-1970s on, engaged in daily reporting and film criticism.

Appointed Media Editor of the paper, he was next Editor of *Filmfare* while continuing as the daily's film critic for 27 years. He reviewed television for *The Economic Times* besides contributing articles to *The Illustrated Weekly of India* and *Femina.* His writing has also featured in *India Today, The Indian Express, The Telegraph,* the international film weekly *Variety* and in *Sunday Observer,* London.

He was film critic for *Mid-day,* Senior Editor of *DNA* newspaper, and National Culture Editor and film critic for *Hindustan Times.* Currently, he is Consulting Editor to the *Deccan Chronicle* media group.

He has translated eminent painter MF Husain's autobiography—*Where Art Thou?*—from Hindustani to English.

He has written the original stories and screenplays for three Shyam Benegal films: *Mammo, Sardari Begum* and *Zubeida.* He wrote the original stories and screenplays and also directed the films *Fiza, Tehzeeb* and *Silsilaay.* He debuted recently as a playwright and director of the stageplay *Kennedy Bridge.* His documentary *The Last Irani Chai* has been screened widely. His second documentary *Smiles and Tears* on Mumbai's street children is under post-production. Presently, he is writing his second stageplay and his first novel.

TWO MOTHERS

AND OTHER STORIES

KHALID MOHAMED

Om Books International

First published in 2012 by

OM

Om Books International

Corporate & Editorial Office
A-12, Sector 64, Noida 201 301
Uttar Pradesh, India
Phone: +91 120 477 4100
Email: editorial@ombooks.com
Website: www.ombooksinternational.com

Sales Office
4379/4B, Prakash House, Ansari Road
Darya Ganj, New Delhi 110 002, India
Phone: +91 11 2326 3363, 2326 5303
Fax: +91 11 2327 8091
Email: sales@ombooks.com
Website: www.ombooks.com

Cover photograph: Zubeida
Courtesy: Khalid Mohamed

Author photograph: Suresh Natarajan

ISBN: 978-93-81607-09-1

10 9 8 7 6 5 4 3 2 1

Printed at Thomson Press, India

Fayazi *ma* for telling me stories without an end...

CONTENTS

ACKNOWLEDGEMENTS

My *shukriyas* go to those I love and those I miss every day of my life. Stories can't be written. They leap out on being provoked, prodded, encouraged. Those who have lent me their ears and empathy, I thank now with a published embrace...

Farouq Rattonsey, the So-what's-happening? friend, the kindest and the most severely critical;

Deepak and Suman Gupta for gifting me their love, their unconditional acceptance, and a home away from home in New Delhi;

Rashid Irani who says, "Sorry, sorry, sorry..." when I am to blame, for the hours at his book-splattered home, and his teashop that was;

Rafique Baghdadi, city historian, for the voluminous books he presses on me, for his sparkling eyes and free consultations on the life and times of Mumbai;

Ajay Mago, my publisher—multi-tasking and yet attentive—for believing in my stories when all the other publishers had their unbargainable don'ts;

Dipa Chaudhuri, my editor, for reflecting creativity and maturity while handling an overreacting brat of a writer—me. And also for a shared passion for *Madame Bovary* and *Notes From the Underground;*

Sonalini Chaudhry, my human spell check;

Deepa Gahlot, for getting me to theatre and back in one piece...and truth be told, for exhorting me to write this collection.

Vajir Singh, my *bua* whom I owe many birthday presents, and he isn't even complaining;

Nilufer Qureshi, for decades of smiles, tears and unwavering friendship;

Suresh Chhabria, my intellectual touchstone;

Chintan Upadhyay who screams murder whenever I procrastinate, and for his art;

Sabir Masani, the tough boy-next-door with a real soft heart;

Karan Desai, my colleague and assistant director who loves theatre more than his life;

Sumi Gupta of London, caring and classy;

Santosh Sivan, the genius who won't stop calling me "Kaalid *bhai*";

Richa Chadha, my *shehzadi,* for calling me, "Sir", "Boss" and when she's feeling especially warm, "Daddy";

Salma of Chandni Chowk, for loving me—her brother—madly, but never saying it;

Sooni Taraporevala for her Mozartian laughter, precious advice on story machinations and Sleater Road affinity;

Ketaki Sheth who actually calls me, "Handsome!" to get me out of an ugly mood;

Aseem Bajaj, for the persistent question, "When are we shooting a movie?";

Baljit Chadha, for his take on some of the stories;

Karan Johar—coffee and sympathy from my Kaaru, always there;

Shah Rukh Khan, for helping me to clean up one...or is two?...of the stories;

Rishi Kapoor, my *jigri dost;* the world can change but not Chintu;

Anil Kapoor, for his straight-talk, humour and undiminished affection;

And the late MF Husain whose short and epic stories are still to be told.

Two Mothers and Other Stories is neither about heroines nor heroes. Besides the two mothers—Fayazi and Zubeida—every other individual is fictional, with a chessboard of qualities.

Two Mothers

Tilting her head like a viewer in a museum, she fades in photographed by his memory, cooing, billing, making all the correct motherly sounds, scooping him up in her slender arms. He can feel the light sensual fuzz, kissing him, caressing him.

One year old, two years old...too much is made of age. It doesn't matter if you die at 72 or 73, 80 or 81. It doesn't matter if he was one, two or three, when she perished. She left him like one would leave an airless room. To this day he isn't sure about when, the moment. Or more to the point, how deep her love was for her son, if it was deep at all. He thinks of her *in extremis:* either she loved him insanely or not at all. He goes on about love-love-maternal-love. He has been told by a psychoanalyst of his acquaintance that when a child is denied love in infancy, it grows up warped, loony tunes, locomotive breath, a jazz rock riff which goes all over the place and can't return to the groove. Can't. Doesn't want to.

With the advance of age, this one-two-three year old is surprised. He inched up to medium height but not to become sullen or morose. He wasn't prone to depression; he could laugh till he had to be stopped. Often he knew not why he was laughing: a bird dropping on a pedestrian's shirt was enough for him to caw-caw. So funny.

He excelled in studies, secured a Master's in Political Philosophy. No stress there, topper at University. If he could top, imagine the acumen of the other dolts, he'd huff to himself, feeling so honest about being aware that he's no big deal. He parachuted into a journalist's job, selected from a shortlist of hundreds. Undiminished gratitude wells for that 'word of recommendation' from a stalwart editor, father of a school friend. Occasionally, the journalist wrote wonderfully—no hyperbole here—his words like embroidery on paper. More often than not, it was another wretched day, words bouncing off his mind like bogus cheques.

He's a writer but he's not a son. It's late. Yet he yearns to be a mother's son. An obedient son. A rebellious son. A mixed-up son, a son, a son. He longs to remove this anxiety surgically. Suture it. Boning up on Sigmund Freud is not mandatory. Anyway, that fellow died in 1939, two decades before he was born. Austria...he dreams of travelling there to waltz perchance. He will not visit Freud's birthplace, nor his fabled study room there. Doesn't want to hear Mozart on the streets either. He just wants to *be* in Austria. Odd guy, doesn't need reasons. No motivations. No furtive agendas. No double life. The nights will be solitude in indigo, cognac lighting a fire in his heart, alone, on the cobbled streets. *Naah* forget that night flight to Vienna. Too much romance attached to those damn cobbles.

Childhood-adolescence-adulthood. That mother of his, always tilting her head at him as if he were an art exhibit. Or so he wants to believe. He has been described as mild-mannered, effete in some ways, his slow-mo drawl so cultivated, so affected. He has tried to speed up his manner of speaking. Only then he's too fast and the idiots ear cock, "What did you say? What? What?" He ignores the boorish what-sayers. The conversations continue.

Now, he's salt-and-pepper, silver streaked. Disappointing that, since he had nursed this delicious fantasy that he is Peter Pan—ageless. Deep worry lines can be handled; he still looks at least ten years younger than he is. Always has. Except that one time when a bank clerk had recommended a senior citizen investment plan. No desperate desire for that extra one—or is it half?—per cent of interest per annum. He did not return to that bank. He's vain. He longs to tell his mother—maddeningly conspicuous by her absence—about the bank android, a clerk blinder than a bat. Mother, mum, mom, mamma, ma, so many variations on you...mum.

Oedipus Rex—been there, read that. "You have an Oedipus complex boy! Grow out of it. If you know you're stalked by that complex, simplify it," he hears himself on silent mode. "You're not alone. So many are in the same boat. Shut up! Just live with it if you can." Damn, not much to learn either from random case studies archived by those doddering institutes of social studies. Human behavioural patterns...can't figure them out. Random patterns. Snag ahead. No one, not even kindergarten kids marvel at hand-made kaleidoscopes anymore. Internet zigzags are more ziggy.

Reading doesn't calm the storm within. Irreparably he is devoured by guilt, the cancerous guilt that he wasn't grateful enough to his mother and to his grandmother, the *nani* whom he called *ma*.

His grandmother had brought him up making him feel like Moses, a child who could have died but was placed in a basket midstream, rescued and leased a life. *Nani,* no no *ma,* even saw *The Ten Commandments* with him at the Regal Cinema. So what if she didn't know the *ish* of English? She graded Charlton Heston "*Behad hi khubsurat!*" She wept when the baby in the basket floated down the studio stream. Her grandson wept to keep her company. He would do that—if *ma* wept, he wept, the two howling as if they were competing to be louder. Laughter Clubs have clicked. Crying Clubs could be as calming. Cathartic. Grandmother and grandson felt noble after crying in orchestrated harmony.

Nani repeatedly reminded him that he wasn't weaned on his biological mother's milk. By some miracle, *nani* had lactated when he was an infant; she had breastfed the sobbing, starving child, while showing him the gaslights of Marine Drive. They clip-clopped on a Victoria, the child, and his surrogate mother who was neither young nor old. She was of indeterminate age.

The 'real' mother—who gave birth to him—was lored to be 18 when she abandoned her son. She had remarried, a Rajasthan maharaja after a day's courtship at the Mahalaxmi Racecourse. Ever since this was revealed to him, the boy had avoided going close to horses. No childhood thrills of pony rides on Chowpatty beach. He didn't hate horses. In fact, he was dumbstruck by the illustrated story book on the travails of Black Beauty. Instead, he had an aversion to mosquitoes. The maharaja had nicknamed him *Khatmal*—bed bug—because he was small. Bloody hell, that damn maharaja. If his mother, yes yes yesssss 'real' mother hadn't left with him, if that raja-maharaja hadn't existed at all, *Khatmal* could have led a normal life. Whether he was small, big or medium, didn't matter now.

Often he congratulates himself for not making heavy weather of the absence of his mother. She could have been a witch, enwrapped in sun yellow chiffon, stinking of duty-free fragrances, smoking an ultra-lite cigarillo. He could have grown up a wastrel deep into booze and drugs. He could have gone over the edge if she were swanning, preening, slapping him hard and barking constant *firmans* to quit home. Home? Whose home? He could have become twisted (a friend calls him eccentric but then so is the friend). Perhaps he would have married, sired a couple of children, led a sedentary life like all the men have in his extended family, living off the rent of ancestral property. So can he but he doesn't know money.

He wouldn't know when to admit and eject tenants from the two empty homes willed to him by dearest *nani*. He would have been in a gutter, castrated, mutilated, were it not for her.

Thank you thank you thank you—can't stop the thank you's for the home, homes. He will glide through the rooms as if in a dream. No sub-letting, no sale. *Shukriya, shukriya, shukriya* in every language.

In any case there *was* that interminable litigation with a truck transport company. Its two partners, bumptious brothers with bovine wives and beastly children, paid ₹ 750 a month for the large apartment which had been selected after much to-ing and fro-ing by *ma*. Eleven months later, the tenants insisted that the apartment was theirs, something about leave and licence rights then. By a sleight of divine intervention, the truck company went bankrupt. Cheating cases were registered by dozens of debtors against the duplicitous brothers. One brother blamed the other for their arrest warrant, lunging at each other's throat. After that the apartment was neither let out nor used but for occasional bouts of afternoon sex with the married woman next door. Her husband was no longer interested in sex, or her, for that matter.

A juvenile streak never left the abandoned and repossessed son. He wondered if his two mothers were watching him orgasm. If so, would they forgive him? He hadn't married because *ma* didn't approve of any girl. If she had, she would have made his wife's life a living hell. Once he had brought home a candidate. Sheena. The two women pretended to like each other, smiled, smiled, smiled. Out of each other's range, both frowned, frowned, frowned. "Won't work, she's cement-tough," Sheena clucked. Her opponent didn't utter a word. Tossed the cool ploy of no comments. Silence meant no consent.

When she organised tea meetings with eligible girls from the various Muslim *mohalla*s, she would hurry up with the ritual. "Terrible, terrible, terrible," *ma* would write off his prospective bride. If he contradicted her with a non-committal, "She wasn't bad. I kind of liked her," she would be outraged, "You are blind. Leave such decisions to me, will you?" He did. *Ma* was manically possessive of the grandson whom she had probably saved from death. Or an orphanage. Or a gangrenous, greedy aunt. So no problems. He was grateful enough to dedicate the rest of his life to her. Marriage, regular sex, *tchah*. Gratitude to *ma* is good good good.

As a school kid, he foresaw himself committing suicide the day his *ma, nani ma,* died. Many moons later, *ma* died after a fall. Slipped while feeding pigeons in a rain-wet corridor. He was reading the Sunday papers. Ever since, he has not been able to read a word on Sundays. The after-breakfast ritual reminds him of her howl, *"Beta, main to gayee."* She didn't recover from the surgery, and would not allow a physiotherapist inside the house—an economy-pack drawing room leading to two matchbox bedrooms. Slow tragedy was about to begin in their two BHK as Mumbai's apartments are termed. He wanted to look after her like his little injured lamb but would race out at the flimsiest pretext, the most common one being he had to replenish her medicines.

She rained filthy abuses. *Ma* didn't want to walk, so she would go plauuunk on the autumnal rust red couch and then plauuunk on an austere white bed. She transmitted the pain to her grandson, her son, a man, a child...who knows? The therapist, her young breasts straining against her T-shirt, smiled with studied benevolence, "Well," she started with the platitude, "We all have to go some day. No one lives forever," and wound up with, "You will have to be patient with your *ma*. Dementia exposes the harsher side of the gentlest creatures on earth." Despite dispensing such logic, the therapist, fever-eyed as she was, didn't return, couriering a terse note instead, "Good luck. I pray for your grandmother's recovery." Who needs notes? Who needs prayers? And why had she called *ma* 'grandmother' now?

When *ma* died in hospital, her mouth shaped into a surprised 'O' to bid farewell, he went numb, but didn't see himself committing suicide. How stupid would that be. She had to go.

Curiously, he felt more hemmed in than free after her body was laid to rest in Sonapur, a confinement aggravated by the shortage of space at the chlorophyll green cemetery. *Ma* would have to share her grave with countless others. A chintzy marble tombstone for her would mean a bureaucratic run-around; he would have to hustle a minister's letter of recommendation. Even then, there was no guarantee that the tombstone would be placed above the remains of her body. He didn't do right by her, even for her grave. He didn't know who would teach him anymore to live. He would have to learn to live without her. No *ma* now.

A woman glued mostly to her New York brownstone loft, Air-India'ed into town. An NRI, a mid-rung writer envious of Jhumpa Lahiri's acclaim, she downed vodkatinis, chin chin, at the Sun 'n' Sand bar, one of her feet squirrelling into the legs of his trousers. For once he didn't shuffle away. He moved his shoe over hers, clumsy clumsy. It wasn't his first time or anything quite ridiculous as that. He laughed suavely, "Just look at the names on the menu. Whisky Frisky, Margarita Drizzledom, Obloody Oblada Mary!" More ha ha. Then she said with the firmness of a führer, "Your *ma*...your grandmother...right?...had a great innings. Now you must do exactly what you want to."

Heil Lady. Let's do it on the road.

"Ha ha, no. Your room's more private."

New York woman switched on iPod reggae in her ocean-blown suite; just see, they are dancing tight like welded incestuous twins. He chortles. The lights are on, there's an element of the cheesy. He feels her cold pudding body against his lean frame. Physically totally incompatible. He is laughing, "This woman is as limp as a Dali clock..." Then the urgent let's-do-it-orgasm-orgasm. Meanwhile Bob Marley's on the speakers. The woman's warming up, better, so much better now. Frisky Whisky. Terrific. Look he has forgotten *ma*. Ditto for the other mother. They have been deleted, erased, exterminated, synonymed.

He's kidding himself. He must tell the two mothers to go away. Leave me women, leave me now, let me be. The NRI woman and he are moving towards mutual masturbation. Performance anxiety attacks him. He comes, she pretends to. She can get no satisfaction, but says, "Wow that was awesome, man...awesome!" *Awesome,* no way. She's fake. She tries another take, purrs as after-sex women are supposed to, "You stud, where were you all my life? See you later."

Marley kept buzzing "Buffalo soldier, buffalo soldier."

He returned home to twin ghosts. The two mothers were inseparable in his memory. He didn't have to peer myopically into the lanes of his imagination; he didn't want to see their profiles accentuated. In any case, most of his dreams were out of focus. Still the son was theirs, no one else's. They didn't return stupidly like Banquo's ghost for a serial gapefest; they resided in him. The two women and he were comfortable in that 2 BHK even if he had it redesigned, reconstructed into a studio apartment, kitchen included, just about. He has more space for himself, and for them. He has persisted in keeping his other apartments tenant-free, can't see anyone occupy his property, *ma's* property.

No triviality here please. He didn't want to forget or exorcise the ghosts of his mothers. On the contrary, he wanted to know more about them. At the outset, more about his biological mother because he hadn't seen her at all. She would just tilt her head at him, an invisible visual. "Do I remember you well? Have I done right by your memory?" he would ask, and then again, "But did you do right by me?"

No right, no wrong. No destiny, no *karma,* no *kismat.* It's all there, the tide of circumstances, events and results. That impels him to know more about his history if there was one of a cindered family tree. His father, somewhere on the other side of the border, Pakistan, didn't arouse his interest. Never never never. The two mothers do. *Abba,* father, was instructed by *ma* with steely resolve, *never ever* to see the boy. He attempted to; it would have been abnormal if he hadn't. He was humiliated. Like those countless treaties between India and Pakistan—ineffectual. Maybe *abba* is dead now, maybe he's a lech with a merry-go-round of a family and mistresses in Lahore, Karachi, Islamabad, Whereverabad. Who cares!

Think of *abba* and he thinks of a father fornicating amidst satin pillows, dragging on an opium pipe. Fuck, now stop being coy, go ahead say it...fuck fuck fuck, the fucker should have reclaimed his infant son. Somehow.

Invariably, he imagined his father with women peach-complexioned, fleshy, crimson valentines for lips. They admire *abba,* his calf-leather wallet, his insatiable libido.

He remembers that *abba* carried a whisky flask in the outer pocket of his woollen, grey-green jacket. He chain-smoked and even offered the little boy a puff. Or was that the son's cynical imagination? Another absence in his life but he did not want to search for more meaning in this one. Too unwieldy, too predictable perhaps. By contrast, the two women appeared, disappeared, appeared like arias of *Four Seasons.* Within him and away, he had to know more about them, yet he was clueless about how to roll the dice.

He merely has his 'real' mother's photographs in their disintegrating old frames, many of them Art Deco with rows of plastic ribbons. He has many photographs of *ma* too but photographs can't speak. He thinks of his relatives—aunts, cousins, uncles, the debris—as a brainless, uncaring mob. They don't talk of the 'real' one beyond a word count; the aunts merely chant Greek chorus-like, "Your *ma,* what a wonderful, wonderful, wonderful woman. Were it not for her..." Oh he would be a stinking corpse, but see here he is, cool, comfortable, eau de cologned.

To change the subject, an aunt over 70, converses with him as if he were a knee-high child, "*Bacha,* today men wear perfume. There was a time...may Allah preserve her in heaven when your mother and I would sprinkle

Evening in Paris ka scent all over ourselves. It came in a dark blue bottle you know...the men would be entranced... not that your mother needed *Evening in Paris*. She was so beautiful." Then she reappraises the abandoned son, "You don't look like her, the same lips perhaps, the same hands..." Stop.

He suspected that his grandmother had serious differences with her daughter but never brought them up within earshot of the brainless aunts. *Ma* had erased the differences, not a trace survived. *Ma* was on self-medication, she had detoxed her daughter out of her heart. He would quiz his *ma,* his *nani ma:* "How could you allow your daughter to sneak off to All India Radio to enter a *ghazal*-singing contest? How could you allow your daughter to audition for a film? For a studio baron's dance opus? How could you allow your daughter to bob-cut her hair...how, how, how?"

To that *ma* would respond with raindrop-sized tears, "You break my heart. She was not of this world; she listened to no one. She won that *ghazal* contest and deposited the ₹ 500 prize money in a bank as if I would have gobbled it up like a *paan*. After a month, that bank closed down. *Kya bolte hein,* bankrupt. And she wept, 'I should never doubt your intentions *ammi*.' That's how it was between us. There was trust. What else can I tell you?"

No more lies, anything but lies.

Emotionally arrested, the son ever since he was in his teens, was sceptical about every story, whether it was narrated by *ma* or the maids, servants or random acquaintances. *Ma* comforted him—the other one had gone away on a secret journey with her maharaja; some enemies were thirsting for the maharaja's blood; the maharaja and she were hiding in the mountains; they would return one fine day with treasure chests of gold, diamonds and pearls—all laden on elephant back. They would kiss him, turn by turn; for him they would fly in the sharpest pair of jeans, tees and belts from America. They would send him to Paris to learn Art, if not to Oxford or Cambridge to study English. He would just have to snap a finger, his will would be done. More generous than Aladdin's genie, instead of three, they would grant him limitless wishes.

Childishly, he believed. Even now under moods of disaffection, he doesn't terminate the fantasy. The unseen mother could still descend from the high mountains—with wishes.

Searches end, puzzles are completed. Not his. He loves his two mothers equally, in contrary ways: one for being a Mysterious Portrait, the other for being Mother Courage. Courage, bombastic that, but shut up, she deserves bombastic. One near-fiction, the other absolute fact. He has no other leads, clues, no reminiscences, no yarns, no more half-truths, no more lies. He has the invisible mother's gold wrist watch; he has *ma's* legacy ensuring a lifetime of indolence if he wants it that way.

The son has a letter, too. It could be the key; it could be yet another lock. He doesn't have the guts to get it read; he doesn't want to but must if he is to complete his story. It is placed in a drawer.

The envelope is strikingly yellow-brown, sepia, yet the ink is as dark blue as a sea in turmoil. A letter from a daughter to her mother: two small, lined pages, written in Urdu, which he cannot read. He has tried all his life not to get the brittle pages read. Like he doesn't spend the ₹ 5,000 that *ma* left in a cupboard before she fell in the corridor. That money is precious, the letter, a dare.

It is his 50th birthday today, a day of decision. He can't prolong the agony, the lingering ache. The letter may be nothing at all, perhaps a polite epistle, perhaps a revelation. Dear mums, should he play roulette? Gamble? He doesn't want to lose, can't. The hurt would be lethal.

He has never celebrated his birthday, because it is as meaningless as that silly suicide resolution. On that day, he visits *ma's* grave where she may or may not be decomposing anymore. The Sonapur cemetery is monsoon green, teeming with beggars offering to water the graves. The assumption is that the bodies beneath will feel cooler, happier. He doesn't accept the offer. Today he leaves the graveyard swiftly, rushing back in a taxi to his apartment, impetuously collecting the letter still in a 4-*anna* cover. He has to do it.

He vends his way to the mosque where he has been invited by the *maulvis* time and again. He would never go, half convinced that the prayers he has formulated in his heart are his purest conversations with his Allah. His *ma* would have liked him to be more religious, perform the *namaaz* and observe the Spartan regimen of month-long *rozas*. She wasn't dogmatic about conventions though. When his school studies overburdened him, she left him to his books. Allah would understand.

Right now, he steps guiltily into the powder-blue mosque. If Allah doesn't understand, an apology would be tendered. He will keep *rozas* next year. Right now, he looks for the *maulvi* who reads the Koran over weekends in memory of his *ma*.

"Could you read this letter for me, *maulvi saab*?" the son says, masking his curiosity.

That letter has to be read. This is as good a time as any other. He wants the two women out of his life. It is not too late. He can still move on, forge new relationships, break free like that song by Freddie Mercury. Kicking himself in the mind for being so juvenile—why think of Mercury now?—he looks expressionlessly at the *maulvi*.

The bent *maulvi* scans the letter. A minute, maybe two elapse. No recognisable emotion on his face, he asks, "Are you sure you want me to read this out to you? Some things are best forgotten. This letter will only bring you grief."

"That is alright *maulvi saab*."

"Listen then."

The letter from his mother to his *ma* reads:

Ammi, aadab.

I hope this letter finds you in good health. We could not speak properly on the phone on Sunday. You are now not accepting my phone calls. You are hurting me very much ammi. *I have done no wrong. You are behaving as if I have.*

I think you have done me wrong...and only in a letter I can tell you why ammi. *I must remind you of what you did because your memory is convenient. It forgets the things you do not have the guts to accept. Remember, please remember I had barely begun to have my periods when* abba *and you got me married off to that man...how old was I? I do not want to think about it.*

Disho and Munni were born...my twin daughters died because you insisted on garlanding them on their first birthday, as if I had achieved some great feat by keeping them alive so far. I asked you time and again not to have a jalsa *for them.*

Doctor Sakholkar had told you that they were delicate, they were running fever. They should have been resting, not being passed around from arm to arm as if they were some toys...toys for you to show off. Yes they were lovely, you were proud of them...but ammi *you don't listen to anyone but yourself. To date you have not accepted the fact that they caught pneumonia because of those foolish wet garlands. Didn't your sisters have enough sense to keep those wet garlands away from them? Didn't you? I asked all of you to let the girls be...but no, you did just what you wanted. You are responsible for my little ones going away...you are guilty. What else can I say?*

But I will say something about my son, my darling, whom abba *and you would not allow to go with me. I have remarried,* ammi, *I have not committed a crime. I had to get away from you.*

This is to tell you in no uncertain words that I want my son back. I will raise him, I will give him the name I want to. He will have every luxury the world has. You cannot give him a mother's love. You are a monster. You ate up my Disho and Munni. I will not let any kind of harm come to my son.

My husband's ADC Bhairon Singh will be coming along with a nanny to collect my son this coming Sunday. Please hand him over. Or else court proceedings will become necessary. Allah haafiz.

Zubeida, once your daughter

The ADC didn't reach Bombay.

She and the maharaja perished in a plane crash, a two-seater. Conspiracy theories abound. Difficult to decode them. Perhaps no one wants to.

Life, and death, must move on.

The *maulvi* did not say a word as the son left the mosque. The face wreathed in a relieved smile, the son returned to his home, to the two women in his life. He loves both. He belongs to them and they to him.

They cannot be evicted.

AS-SALAAM ALAIKUM, MR MINISTER

Cuticura talc, Hazeline vanishing cream, a hint of rouge, sandalwood *attar* and Monkey brand black toothpowder were her beauty secrets. So darlingly the 1960s. Lipstick she detested, asterisking that as a virtue, "I was born with lips painted pink. Why apply all that *laali* on them?" To cloak a near-absent neck, she wore her grey hair long, braided, a lazy snake halting below her hips—or wound into a dinner-roll bun. Her oval chin had the tiniest green tattoo in the world, a microscopic polka dot actually. She couldn't have been a teenager when she was cajoled into a joint tattoo session; her closest friend had convinced her that the dots would remind them of their dreamy days of togetherness. Ineffective. She couldn't remember her friend's name. Maybe she didn't want to.

Fayazi *ma* was fathomless—alternately jocose and morose. She encouraged her only grandson, Adeeb, to call her *ma*. "Your silly parents have gone to party up in the clouds," she would unroll yarns about them fox trotting at exclusive celestial clubs. There were days when Adeeb feared her next volley of laughter and there were days when he would shake her physically, "*Ma,* why are you so sad?" Mad or sad, there was a constant about her: a crisis combatant dwarfing the men of the house, even when it came to physical pyrotechnics.

The cinemascope-wide villa of Mazhar Cassum Abdullah and Fayazi in a secluded land's end of one of Bombay's seven islands, was an open invitation to burglars. The 10-year-old grandson was amazed that there had been no intruders except for a size-zero snake which *ma* had scoffed at, counselling her petrified retinue of domestic helps, "Let it go. If you don't bite the fellow, it won't bite you back." Then one summer night, a weedy young man was seen in silhouette, helping himself to the table clocks, silver antiques, and *ma*'s silk purse containing 100-rupee notes, a gold ring and her ivory comb. Adeeb was lost to the world when her hand muffled his mouth. In a flash, she pounced on the thief with a hockey stick kept by his school satchel. Using the stick as if it were a cricket bat, she was about to get a crack at the thief's skull, when he fell at her feet, pleading, "*Maai baap, maaf karna.* I have two little children to feed. They haven't eaten for days." The wretched fellow's face was swollen, his left eye a black smudge. The old woman stared daggers at him but he did leave with ₹100 for those two children, "You miserable creature. If you are lying, the curse of Allah will be upon you," and a warning, "Don't you do it again."

Mazhar Cassum *nana,* his husky valet and chunky muscular chauffeur had watched the spectacle in silence, certain that Fayazi *ma* would be the hero of the day. Why risk a grapple with the burglar who could have whipped out a Rampuri knife?

Petite and stout she was but on being challenged, she could take on all the wrestlers of the world. About that Adeeb had no doubt. She wasn't educated, and if she couldn't pronounce a word or a brand, she'd make up her own lingo. There was no hiding her yen for the actor, Rajendra Kumar, but she couldn't quite get Ra...jen...dra right. Too tongue-twisty. Frigidaire became *'fezzydear'*, restaurant became *'rasta aunt'*.

Her sister in Delhi and she had devised a code language: men were *'loorey'*, alcohol was *'kurchani'*, and exclamations were *'jhola'*. To disapprove of a man drinking in their presence they would roll their tongues, *"Jhola. Yeh lura to kurchani kurach raha hai."* Adeeb picked up the language merely by listening to *ma*. She'd instruct him to go silent if he was ever asked by a school chum to share his pocket money, *"Koi nessay chownge to nhupka ho jaiyo."* Who coined this language? From where did it originate? Occasionally she would invent tragic excuses for keeping him away from school; his class teacher would be phoned and informed that there had been a death in the family—till the teacher summoned up the nerve to inquire, "Please don't mind but may I ask who has suddenly passed away last night?" It would be another elder sister who had popped it after a *'heart atague'*. The teacher's resigned condolences would be accepted solemnly with a, "*Shukriya*. You are very kind," a pause, "and understanding."

Adeeb wouldn't stop laughing if Fayazi *ma* couldn't remember the brand of her regular soap bar in a store. He wouldn't help her either. She would be amused at her absent-mindedness, play cute with the store clerk, "What are you gaping for, my dear? Just give me that soap used by film stars. One pink, one white...and don't play hanky panky with the bill. I can't add one and one but my boy here, he will check. His name's Adeeb. You know what Adeeb means? I chose that name for him. Means a literary man. Educated! Tip-top! Do you even know the name of the school he goes to? The best in the city, best in India." The store clerk and she would chat about his dilemmas at home for the next 15 minutes. She would promise to pray for him, "Every Friday I will remember you in my *duas*," and leave with one more admirer in her shopping bag.

One day, though, when she showed up at his school, Adeeb wanted the earth to open and swallow him up. Not like the other mothers, crisp and queenly but there she was. Help. He had been given a 'double promotion', which meant he could skip doing his seventh standard. Fayazi *ma* had mixed feelings on the subject. At home, she had glowered, "I smell a conspiracy in this. A student must climb the ladder, one step at a time. Why are they doing this? Why?...I get it. They don't want you to stand first in class every year. I won't have any of this cheating. *You must always be first-class-first. Awwal number!*"

In a red rage, the next morning, shortly after the noon recess, there she was swathed in a white cotton sari imprinted with motifs of corn stalks. Better than the one printed with strawberries and bugle-toting angels. A shudder sprinted down Adeeb's spine. She admonished the Geography teacher, Mrs Indu Karat, that she was wise to her game. Mrs Karat was baffled. Kindly, she led the visitor to the principal's chamber. Adeeb smouldered with anxiety. An hour later, Mrs Karat and *ma* re-emerged looking like soul sisters. *Ma* kissed her grandson, and said theatrically, "Go my son, go. Be victorious in whatever you do. I didn't know you were so clever. I've been told that you can climb any ladder, no steps required." As she hugged Adeeb repeatedly in the corridor outside the classroom, he pleaded, "*Ma*, please go now." As soon as she left, the classroom hooted, "Ladder ladder, you can climb every ladder..." Mrs Karat shushed the boys, and Adeeb was told to pack his books and move to eighth standard. "Baby cry baby, bye bye," the class chorused. Mrs Karat exploded Vesuvius-like, "No indiscipline in MY class. SILENCE, this very minute!"

Nana was quixotic with Adeeb, handing over a lavish *Eidi baksheesh* of ₹1000 one year, and barely registering his *"Eid Mubarak, nana"* the next. *Nana's* moods hinged on his catheter. His urine, dripping into a bottle, was changed frequently. Paralysed on the left side of his body, he could neither come to terms with his immobility nor with the simple fact that his second wife, Fayazi, younger than him by 20 years, was superbly larkish, flying from one end of the villa to another, without a trace of breathlessness or fatigue. "You witch, all you need is a broom to fly. Stop showing off. I can see you can walk. Don't make fun of me," he'd whinge. *Ma* would throw her pretty nose in the air, and hop away, lancing him with, "Don't forget you're 80. If I leave you, it's all over for you." Reminded of his imminent mortality, *nana* would pull angrily at his hookah, "Why do I have to smoke this rot?" and throw a fit for his daily emergency cigarette. Fayazi *ma* would light it and place it between his dark lips, "There! Happy?" Unknowingly, she played her cards wrong.

Since *nana* was acutely aware that Fayazi and her grandson could walk out on him, he kept vacillating over his will. "Do you want me to croak tomorrow? I will put it all in writing—for you, my dearest—as soon as the time is right." Slyly, *nana* wrote his will. The document was kept in the custody of his *khazanchi* Parveen Mehta, whose silence was bought by leaving him a sum of ₹ 1 lakh in the will. The bulk of the estate, adding up to crores, was willed to the caboodle of his sons and daughters from his first wife, scattered across the globe. He was particularly generous to Wahid, settled in London, and to Osman in Karachi. And what do you think, peanuts for Fayazi, and discarded hollow shells for the grandson: ₹ 25 lakhs and ₹ 50,000 *respectively.* Even the sycophant trader, Muljibhai, who supplied tins of *asli ghee* from Porbandar was to be richer by ₹ 50,000.

The villa was to be handed over within a fortnight—to the Estate Duty department for valuation. "What a swine! My tears haven't dried and I have to hear this. Mazhar, may you go straight to hell," Fayazi *ma*'s unshakeable love for her husband had been betrayed. How would she live now? How would she pay for her grandson's education? Oho. That could be managed. He was about to join college, he'd get some scholarship or the other. The unkindest cut of all—how would she cough up the advance tax money on the to-be-inherited ₹25 lakhs? Beg, borrow or just tell those *taxwalla*s that she wouldn't be able to pay up till she got her measly slice of the cake. No, they'd want a slice of the slice well before...what a mess. Her worst suspicions had come true. Mazhar had never lost regard for his first wife; her *maqbara* was the grandest at the Marine Lines *kabrastan*. He had left instructions with that *asli ghee* idiot to be buried next to her. So what was Fayazi for the last 20 years and some more? A glorified companion? An exalted nursemaid? A rare bed romp? Often, Mazhar Cassum would taunt her for her modest background—"Behave. Or I will dump you back in that filthy chawl where you once lived with your brother."

A *maulvi* had brought a proposal for the spinster. The groom was filthy rich; Allah would see the rest fell into place. Had it? Who knows? Wonderful, *saala* Mazhar, see you some day in hell. Till then, what has to be done needs to be done.

Nana's death was clockwork, almost pedestrian. On October 5, 1968, he developed a high temperature, wheezed over his hookah, and was carried to his mechanically operated bed in the most austere room of the villa. He was partial to white and green—the large room was painted a shade of sea green; half the walls were cemented with square white tiles. His children, as old if not older than Fayazi, descended on the villa like parrots on rotting guavas. The grandchildren were kept away from the cantankerous old man who could have reviled and insulted them in his stupor. After a week of furrowed-brow inspections by three physicians, Koran readings by three *maulvis*, and three nights on an oxygen tank, *nana* was off to the pearliest gates this side of a mob of oysters.

To start with, Fayazi *ma* howled in grief, then calmed down steadily but surely, and faced her stepchildren, "What plans do you have for the house, the servants, the silver ware, and for my child and me. Where do you expect us to go?" She *had* to know. They didn't want to. Osman smirked, "We hear *abba* has bought you quite a lot of property. Go there."

She got the drift, and moved with her child to a tumbledown house on rent in a congested area of the city. The landlady was an acquaintance. No concessions were made in the monthly rent, but within two hours, three rooms were opened up for *ma* and her bewildered child, who trundled along uncomplainingly.

He couldn't understand his feelings after *nana*'s burial at the *kabrastan*. Would he miss the eccentric old man? Or would he curse him for leaving them homeless? He had been permitted to throw a clump of earth into the grave. At that moment, he had felt awful; in the evening he had warbled a tragic film song to the high heavens. He was affected. *Ma*, though, had the gift of speedy recovery.

The rooms were a shelter, the neighbours a godsend, welcoming them with smiles and fresh-out-of-the-kitchen *daal, chaawal* and *achaar* till the new entrants could obtain a gas stove connection. The illicit liquor den, round the corner, threw up a nose-clenching stench that *ma* and Adeeb would just have to get used to.

To her credit, Fayazi *ma* called for Sunday prayers in memory of the old codger who had left her as a woman of no means. Adeeb dutifully caught a local train to his opening terms at college, never fussing about the absence of the chauffeured big black Dodge, in which he once whirled round the city haughtily.

Adjustments made, life was reaching a placid plateau when a tax notice was delivered to *ma* by Parveen Mehta. A portrait of misery, Mehta said she would have to shell out ₹ 5 lakhs and pronto—within the month's end—or she would be fined, imprisoned, worse. "Do they expect me to sell my body on the streets?" Fayazi *ma* thundered, offering Mehta a thimble-sized cup of tea.

He muttered, "Madame you can do that but what about me? I don't even have a body to sell. I was banking on the money *seth saab* has willed to me. I served him for so long..."

Ma was in no mood to humour a man in a minor predicament. She locked the notice in an almirah and got busy.

Three days later, Adeeb and *ma* were on their way to New Delhi in the early morning Janata Express. Adeeb fussed. "Be good, my boy, be good," she warned that with his fussbudget behaviour on the train, her bronchial cough was likely to act up. She even coughed a demonstration sample and chastised him, "Do you want me to die? No, you don't. So take the good with the bad. Allah will provide us with money—*dher saare paise*—for a good life some day. Just you wait."

"What about the tax? Will your sister give you a loan? Is that why we're going on this dirty train to Delhi?"

"*Woh saali?* She'll drink the last drop of my blood but won't lend me a *dhhela.* Your *ma* has another plan."

Fayazi *ma* didn't reveal any plan; she didn't have one. She was simply bluffing so that the worry wart of a grandson wouldn't fret.

When the train reached Mathura in the morning, she reminded the sleep-deprived boy, "Once, when we were at this station in the Frontier Mail...in our first-class coupé, you had said, 'It's so cold I've frozen into a *kulfi.*' That was so sweet."

Adeeb was overcome with sadness. *Ma* was still the man of the house. He was a teenager but he couldn't suddenly graduate from college, snag a job, come home running with his pay packet and sob, "This is for you, *ma*." That happens only in those crummy movies.

True to her promise, she kept coughing incessantly. As the train pulled into Nizamuddin Railway Station, she gulped down a bittersweet syrup. Adeeb gently massaged her back. Two women in the clogged compartment, with infants in arms, told Fayazi *ma*, "Your son really loves you."

❧

The plan was set in motion. At the home of Fayazi *ma*'s younger sister in Darya Ganj, she completed all the expected *salaams* and *duas*, and turned solemnly to her brother-in-law, Saleem, "I need an appointment—today if possible—with Mr Morarji Desai."

"What? How's that possible? Have you lost your mind? You know how Delhi is...nothing can be done here without influence..."

"...or money."

Saleem contacted his neighbourhood's local councillor. The fact that *nana* had contributed to the Congress election funds generously over the years was the clinching factor. The councillor was paid ₹ 2,000, the appointment fixed three days later.

Monday, Raisina Hills' Secretariat Building, North Block, 9 a.m. *sharp.*

Fifteen minutes had been allocated to the old lady from Bombay who, in fact, had been very graceful whenever the Finance Minister had dropped by to discuss election strategies with Mazhar Cassum *saab.* Adeeb, back then still a little boy, had taken an instant dislike to Mr Desai who had refused to sign his autograph book: signature granted only to those donning *khadi.* "Strictures are strictures," the politician had looked disapprovingly at the boy in his tweed blazer, woollen trousers, flannel shirt. Only *khadi,* please.

Magpie-*ma* chattered on with her sister, keeping Adeeb at a distance. He really didn't mind; he would wander off to the Jama Masjid or explore Connaught Place. *Ma* described the sense of liberation she felt on becoming a widow. Now she was answerable to none but herself. She didn't have to race to her lord and master at the summons of a mini-brass bell kept on his wicker side-table. That bell was a nightmare. If she was washing her face, she would rush to him, soap faced.

Three days flew by. Monday morning, Adeeb's heart was a roll of drums. At the *masjid,* he had prayed, "Allah, please let this tax problem be cleared...somehow or the other...and one more thing, please let me do well at college. I owe that to *ma.*"

The sun hadn't come out that morning. *Ma* didn't reach out for Cuticura, sandalwood *attar* and Hazeline vanishing cream. She was grim; her sister and brother-in-law were pessimistic; the boy was neutral. If he thought too positive, he conjectured, the result would be negative. The tax notice patted and smoothened into her black velvet purse, Fayazi *ma* was on her marks. During the taxi ride she was set, and on reaching North Block, it was go. "Allah, you are the only saviour of the helpless," she whispered, before entering the wondrous, wood-panelled office of the minister.

The place exuded power. The secretary looked at the motley foursome testily and asked them to sit on the bench outside. "It is very cold there," Fayazi *ma* interrupted. "Think of the boy, he'll fall ill. As it is he has a temperature." On cue, the boy attempted to look frail and ill. Condescendingly, Fayazi *ma* and her grandson were allowed to occupy the tanned leather sofa in the minister's ante-chamber. Protocol forbade the sister and brother-in-law partaking of the privilege. The meeting was for one person; the secretary logged it as one and half—one woman and one boy. It was five to 9 a.m. Half an hour ticked by. *Ma* was reciting prayers under her breath. At 9.35 a.m. the secretary allowed Fayazi *ma* and Adeeb, wearing a defiant tweed blazer, to enter the minister's chamber.

Impressive. Adeeb couldn't take his eyes off the mahogany desk, the oil portraits of Gandhi and Nehru, the thick maroon-cream-blue carpet and rust drapes. Fortuitously, Mr Morarji Desai didn't remember Adeeb but after answering her *as-salaam alaikum* with *walaikum salaam,* he did not stand on ceremony with *ma.* The schooner-sized, inscrutable Desai, however, did pause to tell the secretary to send in three cups of tea. "Two teas," he corrected himself, "and a *mosambi* juice for the boy."

Ma expressed her deep gratitude, "That is so thoughtful. My child, my grandson actually but he's like my own, needs all the vitamins he can get. Nowadays, we don't know where our next meal is coming from."

"Don't think I am a fool, Fayazi. I have gone through your files. You're a rich woman," the minister tripped her at the very first move.

"Morarji *bhai...saab*...no no. If you read the file carefully, you will see that I will get my share only after all the taxes have been cleared and the probate has been obtained. I have only one thing to beg of you...in my eyes you are a munificent benefactor, a messiah of the oppressed."

"Come to the point," the minister commanded.

"Please let me pay the tax after I have been given my share from the will."

"Why can't you pay the sum now? You are the widow of a very wealthy man. You must have jewellery, cash... liquid assets."

"May Allah snatch me away from the face of this earth," *ma* was charging into high dramatics now, "I have nothing. Zero. Strange are the ways of men...of course you are an exception *bhai*...they don't care what happens to their wife after they are gone..."

Tea was served. Adeeb wouldn't touch the juice. He wanted to pummel Mr Desai right there and then for making *ma* grovel. Imagine, she had said *'beg of you'*. How could she? Sugar cubes stirred noiselessly, the conversation resumed.

Mr Morarji Desai was in a hurry to conclude the meeting, "See Fayazi. I had high regard for Mazhar Cassum *saab*. He was a very good man."

"The best, Morarji *bhai*, the best."

"And your intention today is to plead on behalf of his son from Karachi. That Osman fellow, isn't it?"

Startled, Fayazi squealed, "May all the devils lash me with whips. No, not at all, Sir."

"The man is a suspected espionage agent. We cannot take a lenient view of his case. His entry to India has been prohibited."

"*Wah!* That is justice indeed, *bhai*," *ma* emphasised. "Send him to the gallows."

"I see. Then you are in agreement with me."

"200 per cent. I will write it in blood and give it to you on paper if you want."

Adeeb watched his grandmother scoring but on irrelevant points. How would she come back to her tax imbroglio?

"I do not want to take up more time Morarji *bhai*."

"The meeting is over, then. Good Day."

"But what about the tax? I cannot pay it till I get what is due from the will."

"I cannot do anything about that."

"If you want Morarji *bhai,* you can move mountains."

Adeeb saw the Himalayas move but the minister remained as still as a pond.

"Fayazi. It is not within my power to waive off or postpone tax payments...I am sorry."

'Sorry' was the catalyst. Fayazi *ma* pulled out a cheap handkerchief from her purse, shoved it under her nose, and commenced a howl which shook the chamber's wooden panel. Adeeb thought he saw the drapes billow in sympathy. The sour-faced secretary rushed in. The boy grabbed the glass of *mosambi* juice nervously and Morarji *bhai* stood transfixed. At the outset of her marathon howl, he had turned his back to her. When she wouldn't stop her high-pitched sobs, he grew alarmed. Somehow he managed to console her, "Don't cry Fayazi. Everything will be alright."

Between sobs, she stammered, "B...b...but ho... wwwwww?" She wouldn't stop. The minister looked at Adeeb for suggestions. The boy stood silent, the glass of juice trembling in his left hand.

"Are you a lefty?" Mr Morarji Desai tried to change the subject.

"No he isn't!" Fayazi *ma* took a break. "And he won't ever be able to study...to write with his left hand or right...

we are ruined, we will be on the streets," she informed her handkerchief. Encore!

"Give her some water...have some tea, Fayazi," the minister sounded like a doctor.

A moment's silence, and then Fayazi *ma* flooded the chamber with another tide of tears. Adeeb observed keenly—whimpers are a prelude, sobs are the starters, the howl with eyes letting loose dammed tears are the main course, followed by more contained wet hiccups, a negotiable abatement and then a full-on repetition *ad infinitum*. *Ma* had wept a token quota of tears at her husband's funeral, pumping up the volume when his body was carried by the men out of the villa. Today, it was no-hysterics-barred. This crying fit was unlike any expression of grief Adeeb had ever witnessed. How would it end?

A well-timed howl did it. It had to be stopped.

The minister barked at the secretary, "What are you gaping for? Get a handkerchief. Paper tissues...anything. Water." He placed his hand over *ma's* shoulder, then thumped her back gently, "Please stop, please stop. I'll do the needful."

More tears. The secretary rushed in with a handful of paper tissues, thrusting them at the minister who hissed, "Why are you giving them to me? Give them to her. Fayazi, relax. I have said I will do the needful."

"Needful is not enough. I need your letter right now," *ma* was limping back to normal.

"Very well, fine, relax. I will issue a letter to the tax commissioner in Bombay. You should be exempted from paying the tax..."

"Yes?..."

"...till you receive your amount from the will. Right?"

"Perfect."

"It will take me 15 minutes to get it done. Wait here, please. Some water? Tea? It must have become cold. Coffee? Juice?"

"Nothing, nothing, just the letter Morarji *bhai,*" she was about to launch into sobs again.

The minister hurried out of the room with the secretary. Fayazi *ma*'s wet eyes followed their trail. She cocked her ears—yes he was dictating the letter for her. From a half stoop, she sat straight up, grabbed the glass of juice from the wide-eyed Adeeb and drank it one gulp. The tears ended as abruptly as an unseasonal cloudburst.

Then clutching her wet handkerchief, half-crying and half-smiling, she winked at her grandson, her child, "See what a woman's tears can do."

Tehmina from Bandra

Izzath had done the unspeakable. His name meant honour. He had dishonoured it. The whispers intensified into an operatic cymbal-clashing crescendo. He should have never been anointed with such a name. Too much of a burden for anyone to carry for a lifetime.

He had secretly married Tehmina at the civil registrar's. He is 32, can you imagine? Before the flash marriage, the Muhammad Haji Majid family had believed he was a saint who had elected a life of celibacy as unobtrusively as a sparrow which flitters alone on a window ledge.

The bride was older. Who knows, about 35? Not beautiful, attractive or even presentable on the scales used for judging an entrant to the ancestral Mubarak Bungalow, illuminated by an almost Mediterranean sunshine from the lacteal mornings to the ginger-soda evenings.

The bungalow was at the foot of Malabar Hill, Mumbai's abiding real estate paradise. The municipal sign, navy with firm white lettering, christened the road as Narayan Dabholkar. Izzath had spent much of his life there. The Salamat Muhammad Haji Majid clan hardly ever noticing his departures to Panchgani where he managed a modest boarding and lodging hotel—it offered a bed, narrow and coffin-like and a breakfast of tea and biscuits, sweet and salty. Izzath made some money for his upkeep but not enough to prevent him from stammering requests for a loan of ₹100, maybe ₹200, to keep himself in filter-tipped cigarettes and the occasional taxi fare. "He goes by the 122 bus route," his aunts, cousins, and, at times, his mother would grouse, "and lies to us that he travels by taxi."

Tehmina lived in a bylane of Bandra. That is how for the first time back in the early 1960s, I heard of the suburb destined to be called the Queen of the suburbs. A lack of talent for memorising dates hampers me from reporting the precise month, day and the year of the Izzath-Tehmina civil marriage which rocked the Salamat Muhammad Haji Majid family, like a Jimi Hendrix guitar blast. All I can remember is that I could not participate in the bungalow's in-bred gossip. Lit up by malarial fever I was confined to a tall four-poster bed. There were days when I burnt like fire and nights when I felt as if I'd been shoved into Mubarak Bungalow's cranky, going-to-pieces refrigerator which was never replaced because Salamat Muhammad Haji Majid—the nonagenarian patriarch of the household—was on par with Silas Marner.

Salamat *seth saab*'s skinflint ways were legendary. *Seth saab* was affixed to his name. If his children made the mistake of calling him *abba,* they'd receive a sermon on how he had struggled—single-handedly—to rescue the family's floundering business empire. *Seth saab* it had to be, no arguments. And no lavish expenses. He is said to have instructed the chauffeur to bump the family car, a dilapidated Wolsely, against a wall, any wall, so its fender would dent. The insurance company would get it repaired, adding while at it a fresh coat of black paint which the jalopy badly needed. That was the clan's mercantile cunning.

When the men were at home, silence was mandatory in Mubarak Bungalow. Conversations were conducted in whispers. It was advisable neither to be seen nor heard. Salamat *seth saab*'s temper could be ignited by a mosquito which he couldn't swat. He would rail against his seven sons for being hopelessly talentless, incapable of much else but stuffing their bellies. The women were tongue lashed when a *dupatta* did not cover their foreheads piously. Head cooks trembled when it was decreed that the *yakhni pulao* was extra-salty. And there I was, the grandson who was neither loved not detested. Salamat *seth saab* allowed himself two wives and an equal number of mistresses, *discreetly,* in Delhi and Hyderabad. Halima, his first eminently fertile wife, rapidly harvested 12 children. Then he married Sabira while Halima was alive but febrile, diagnosed with breast cancer.

My mother was the only child born to Salamat and his second wife Sabira. Perhaps he was abstemious with my grandmother Sabira although I can swear I once saw him grabbing her hand and moving it on his crotch. Grandmother didn't protest.

So there I was, *chaud* and *froid*, in bed, hoping someone would sit by me, talk to me, narrate a story maybe, or take the trouble of switching off the radio station which played the same songs by Mohammed Rafi, Jim Reeves, Mohammed Rafi, Jim Reeves, over and over again. Now a Rafi song again. I had heard it so often that I wasn't hearing it, when Tehmina entered the room, complexion of breakfast cereal, pockmarked, draped in a butter yellow saree, bespectacled and a smile that pleaded, "At least you can be my friend. No one else wants me here."

With unsuspected bravado, Izzath had brought her home. The bride spoke in murmurs. By stark contrast, the other women of the household pumped up the volume, as soon as Salamat *seth saab* and his male litter left for work, the Buick, Wolseley and Studebaker rumbling out like army tanks from the garages, through the trellised gates. Izzath and Tehmina had been grudgingly allocated a room away from the sea view. A window looked out at the tentacles of a mango tree, and the manicured garden's patch of cecilias and snapdragons. She had stepped out of the room warily to meet a boy inflamed with fever.

Tehmina touched my forehead, her be-ringed finger an icicle. She continued ingratiatingly, "Hello, I'm from Bandra." She could have been from Mars.

Bandra was regarded as a distant suburb in through the 1950s and much of the '60s even though the traffic couldn't have been too dense then. A bus ride would take maybe 40 minutes to cross the Mahim Masjid. Today the ride would take...? Don't even hazard a guess.

No point harping on distances, metro development, the passage of time and more such etc. The point is Tehmina was different.

Women in the Salamat Muhammad Haji Majid estate were unhappy or unhappier. They found fault with the mince marinated by Edward Fernandes the cook, heckled Dattu the gardener for stealing drumsticks from the tree even when he didn't, and looked upon Tehmina as yet another encroacher in their loveless paradise. "*Tauba tauba, Allah maaf kare.* He did not have the decency to marry a Muslim girl," the women shook their heads before praying with beads. They slunk away whenever she entered or left any room to mutter, "Must be a temptress in bed. *Besharam!*"

My fever subsided in the month of May—summer holidays. So Tehmina was a conveniently and quickly appointed friend. She would sit me down on a wrought iron bench, painted moss green, in the large and leafy backyard garden. We were not to be seen together by the other women; they would accuse her of poisoning my mind. They would not understand if I were to correct them, that she was synopsising the plot of *Treasure Island,* reading pages from Anne Frank's diary and excerpts from poems which I didn't understand. I still have the book of Rainer Maria Rilke's poems she left behind. Even today, I remember her reading:

Path in the garden, deep as a long drink,
Gently in soft branches gathering force and then gone.
Oh and the moon, the moon, the benches almost
Blooming from its slow approach.

The silence, how it throngs. Are you awake up there?
Starry and full of feeling the window faces you.
Hands of the winds transpose to your near countenance
The remotest night.

Tehmina was an English Literature student who couldn't graduate from St Xavier's College. She had to leave college midway to work as a lawyer's secretary, a pool typist, and vended home-made confectionery till she met Izzath during a visit to Panchgani where her aged parents spent the last days of their lives in a sanatorium.

"Do you like Izzath?" I asked, amazed. Where on earth did that question come from?

"I love Izzath," she smiled, "and no one else."

"What about me?"

Laughter and then she said, "Go to your *nani.* She'll be upset if she finds out that you've been spending so much time with me."

"Why?"

"I don't know but listen my friend, Izzath and I will be going away soon."

"What!"

"*Seth saab* has bought us a house in Pali Hill. I'll be back in my old neighbourhood, happy to be in Bandra. We'll be leaving soon. Maybe in a week or two."

"No, you can't, not till my holidays are over. What'll I do without you?"

"You can come and visit. Now will you go, please?" she said, more a command than a request.

Pali Hill in those times was like being banished to the Andamans & Nicobar Islands for life imprisonment. I made it clear to my grandparents that I would continue my friendship with Tehmy Aunty.

Salamat *seth saab,* ever intuitive about discovering some use even in the most futile circumstances, gave his assent, "Why not? Her English is good, she can give you English tuitions. We will pay her something."

On a clammy Sunday morning, two Ambassador taxis transported Izzath and Tehmina to Pali Hill. One carried their suitcases and books. The other carried the couple who didn't look back except once quickly to wave back to me.

To plug the sudden vacuum, she left some of her books in my room. About the plainly bound volume of poems, she reasoned, "You will enjoy Rilke when you grow up."

⁂

The Pali Hill apartment was in a housing colony, its walls the shade of burnt caramel, fronted by green bushes and shade-bestowing oaks. The Bandra hills were thickly tree lined. To an extent, some of its stretches still are. The one-room apartment was barely functional but whenever I was there for my tuitions—invariably on Sundays—it was the grandest palace in the world.

From glass *barni*s Tehmina would serve *bhakra*s. She'd *shabash* my appetite when I wolfed down her *saas ni macchhi, kolmi no patiyo* and *dhandaar*.

As the days sped by, Izzath became less visible and Tehmina's calmness more pronounced. I was to learn later that he blamed her for taking him away from the Muhammad Haji Majid estate on Malabar Hill where he had grown up, and from his mother Zainabbi—"After all, she is my mother." Tehmina didn't retaliate. Presumably she thought he was justified in whatever he said, whatever he did, never mind if he shot arrows at her heart.

Tehmina and Izzath had been barely married for a year. Already it was obvious even to a child that they had irreconcilable differences. The Majid women must have cackled, "So he tired of her after a few days. After all how long can any woman hold on to her man in bed? He must have realised she's a gold-digger. *Allah bachaaye aisi auraton se.*"

Tehmina—my Tehmy Aunty—subsisted. She taught regular hours at a Bandra Montessori school. Salamat *seth saab* would give me an envelope with ₹ 300 every month for the English tuitions. Not that she gave me any regimented tuitions. She'd talk of the books she liked, read out Rilke, an obsession perhaps, and whisk me off to New Talkies for a morning show, an eclectic bunch ranging from Jerry Lewis and The Three Stooges to the Dilip Kumar weepies. Hitchcock's *Psycho* was showing there too. With the complicity of the usher I was smuggled into my first 'adults only' experience. Thrilling. She wasn't much of a story-teller really; she couldn't ever make up one. She would read out the keeeooww-splaaaash words in comic book balloons and had me hooked on to the ongoing adventures of Superman and Lois Lane. "Now, there's a great love story," she'd roll her eyes.

Tehmy Aunty felt at home in Bandra. Curiously though, she didn't mingle with the neighbours, preferring long walks on the Carter Road seafront, then devoid of stocky high-rises. She would dream about gatecrashing into Dilip Kumar's house and chatting movies with him. "But that...that Ahsaan Khan guards his brother as if he were made of gold," she grumbled once on being shown the door. "I'm Dilip Kumar's greatest fan in the world," she had rhapsodised. The tragedy king's brother had responded with a monosyllabic, "So?"

The bungalows, many of them with their colonial architecture, fascinated her. Her early Sunday mornings were reserved for the market where fish was brought in from Calcutta. Or she would hop over to meet her closest buddy, Betty Mendonca, at a pebble's throw away from her colony. The two would guzzle beer on Sunday afternoons but I wouldn't be allowed half a sip. "Grow up and we'll see," Betty would promise petulantly.

❧

The Izzath-Tehmina love story ended. Formally.

"He's not coming back from Panchgani," she announced, "and I refuse to go there. It's over."

"Why?"

"Sometimes love stories just end."

"Has he found someone else?"

"Who knows?" she said, without bringing up a word against her husband. "The only thing I know is that I will have to come to meet your grandparents and tell them that Izzath is no longer with me."

Silence. In retrospect, I cannot understand what made me say the next few words, "Please don't come to that house ever again."

She looked at me with new eyes and cried a little. If she hadn't I would have been surprised. "You're right. I don't owe anyone any explanation. You understand."

"What will you do?"

"Nothing. I'll stay here, I like it here. You come here and visit, *hanh*. Don't forget."

❧

I was prevented from visiting Bandra on Sundays. With time, I forgot about Tehmina because I had no choice. Or did I? Once Izzath and she were officially separated, she was taboo for the clan sequestered in Malabar Hill's Mubarak Bungalow.

I had no reason to return to Bandra. Not for years. When I did, the door of her apartment was locked. The neighbours said she had just upped one day, and left. Never to return.

Whenever I pass by the colony, now painted in shades of chocolate, I don't have the courage to check if she ever returned. Was the lock to her apartment ever opened?

If Tehmina isn't there, I won't be able to say sorry for abandoning her, for forgetting her. I want her to be there. In melodramatic tradition I want to seek forgiveness.

If she isn't, what do I return to? ...The first page of the book of Rilke's poems she left behind:

Forget, forget, and let us live now
Only this, how the stars pierce through
Cleared nocturnal sky; how the moon's whole disk
Surmounts the gardens.

To Miss Mordecai With Love

He must have been enchanted the way he was with the expensive pop-up fairytale books from England or with the fair lady under a parasol on the Quality Street tin-box of caramel toffees. So British.

She was a bunch of roses, the pensive Victorian girl emblazoned on a box of cream crackers. She taught English grammar. He looked enviously at the blotchy red copy of Wren & Martin glued to her hand. If wishes were magic he would have become that book.

She grew in his memory, no longer a fairytale princess. He is middle-aged now but hasn't budged from her classroom. He can touch her lips, scarlet as in a Rembrandt canvas. He could gaze at her knee-length *frock*—a one-piece buckled *dress* was called that. The taffeta fabric was brighter than Van Gogh's sunflowers. And her hair cascaded to her waist, a waterfall straight out of Gauguin's Tahiti.

With distance, she became art.

Dream-wrapped boy, dream-wrapped man. The first cut is the deepest like the scar on his wrist. He had jabbed it with a lead pencil to sense how that felt. It didn't hurt, just went inside the flesh and popped out, leaving a blue-black ring that faded with age. He can see it, just about, but her he can see without any mist of time playing tricks.

She was a vision. More than 20 of the 30 boys in the fifth standard, Section B, of Cathedral and John Connon were in love with Miss Mordecai. On Mondays at the Anglo-Saxon school, they brought her polished apples, brandy chocolates, baskets of peaches. He never brought her anything. She would look at him skulking away to the third-row bench. Then she would nod at him but he couldn't read her face. He was sure she expected a gift that would beat all those chocolates, cakes, honey jars the boys routinely placed on her desk, making it resemble a kiddy bazaar. Miss Mordecai accepted all the gifts because it would have been rude not to. "Oh, how sweet of you," she would say absent-mindedly to the boys in white knee-length shorts, white shirts and dark purple striped ties.

Javed Arif dreaded Monday mornings. That school room was a prison; he had been sentenced there without a fair trial. An unfriendly cloud would descend and reside over him till the bell rang. A brass clang-clang-clang. Her class, all of 45 minutes, the most agonising stretches of his life, would be o...v...e...r. He counted every slow tick of his watch, a unisex dial once worn by his mother when she was in school. His heart leapt up gymnastically as soon as Miss Mordecai sashayed out of the room. Then Miss Daniel would march in militantly, her colourless maxi-skirt sweeping the floor like an angry broom.

No gifts were placed on Miss Daniel's desk. Not even a pin or a needle, or a smile by the boys who battled slumberdom while the history teacher babbled on about world wars, armistices and treaties. Hey lady, get a life. He was as indifferent to Miss Daniel as he was to Mathematics. She was undemanding, she'd talkfest and march out on the bell's first clang. No personal equations there.

Javed loved Miss Mordecai. She was so demanding, so hot. He also hated her; she made him feel inadequate. Hell, he wanted to buy the moon and stars for her, not freeload fruit from the home's cavernous refrigerator. How unimaginative was that. He would draw her sketches over the weekend, his fingers helplessly elongating the frock. Erased once, twice, a quick line supplanted, the ankle would be covered. "Miss Mordecai, please don't show your devastating knees, ankles, arm dimples to anyone but me, please," he'd plead with the sketch which was meant to be her but invariably ended up looking like the army general, Miss Daniel. He was insanely possessive. And no one was allowed to share that secret. Monologues merely buzzed inside him till he switched them off. Shut up, go away.

Then one extra-strong monsoon day, the school was almost empty. Students, teachers, who welcome city-crippling downpours stayed home. After class, Miss Mordecai invited him to the staff room.

4.05 p.m. The school bus would be running behind time. Her fiancé, a Mr Dexter, would be late in picking her up on his antique motorbike, that junk heap of a *phatphati.* Javed was apprehensive about the invitation; she would give him a dressing down perhaps, reprimand him for the moony looks he flung at her like darts at a board. "Breathe normally you dumbo," he drew the thin floral curtain open, and was shocked. She was smoking a cigarette, smoke from the filter tip curving up into a question mark. *His* Miss Mordecai smoking, *actually smoking?* No, no, no, God take her away from this earth, whip her, force her to quit smoking. She was positively *evil.* Suddenly, it seemed to rain harder. He imagined the sound of thunder, flash stabs of lightning.

Angel-turned-witch was alone in the staff room; they were alone. The daffodil-printed curtains swayed wildly, sprayed by rain.

"You can keep secrets, can't you?" she asked immediately extinguishing the weed in a saucer and flicking the butt out of the window. Without waiting for an answer, she concluded, "Of course you can. Don't tell a soul that you caught me sneaking a little smoke."

"YESSS MISS!" he shot back like a loyal soldier, surprised that he didn't think of her as a vamp at all.

Snafu sorted. She fixed her oceanic blue eyes on him. He wanted to swim in them, plunge into their depths, never to return. He wanted to just linger in them for the rest of his life, her life, their lives. "Idiot, fool, you stale pastry," his thoughts raced in multiple directions, "so many books and movies talk tragically of being infatuated with the school teacher. You are different. Boy grow up, be cool. Why are you staring at the light valentine-shaped mole dancing on her chin? Stop staring at the other mole at the base of her neck, just below her thin silver chain. STOP. If you touch that mole she will disappear."

Miss Mordecai interrupted his interior monologue, "Look, I know you feel awkward every Monday because you don't get me anything. That's perfectly okay. The others are just trying to gain my attention. You *get* my attention, anyway...*child.*"

"Child? No way. How dare she! Slap her, stomp out of the room, tell the entire world that she smokes a hundred cigarettes, that she's a nasty number, does horribly unmentionable things with Mr Dexter, lures kids into her parlour, horrendous spider woman with a web. You don't want anything more to do with this ...this bitch. She can go to hell...tell her, tell her to GO TO HELL," Javed's head was close to exploding. No, no, this couldn't be happening to him. He applied the brakes. He didn't know what possessed him next, but suddenly he found himself adoring her, "I have to forgive her every fault, major or minor. She's *miiiine,* she's adorable." Miss Mordecai must have called him a *child* to be chummy. She didn't really mean it. She regarded him as an adult, which is why she had called him today. Solo special attention. He had to touch her hair, her neck, that silver chain, that mole on her chin, gasp, perhaps the other mole too, at the base of her neck. He wanted to kiss her, to understand what a kiss means. Kids in the class boasted of kissing girls. He had seen his sister, a gangly freckled freak, kissing a boy, two boys in turn, then together.

He had frequently rehearsed a speech for Miss Mordecai for that magic day when he could talk to her, when he could touch her. Elocution time now. "Miss Mordecai, this has to be our secret. *Can* I tell you something?"

Half-amused, half-startled, she corrected him, "You mean *may* I tell you something?"

He rushed on, "*May* I...may I? I am sorry I have never brought you a gift on Mondays. That is because I don't want to gift you any old stuff. I am waiting...one Monday, some day, I will give you gold, diamonds, pearls and rubies. Many, many diamonds. I will give you perfumes, I will give you great big beautiful carpets and...one day, I swear I will buy you a great big car. You'll sit in the backseat; I'll drive you around the world. Then I'll buy you a train, an airplane...anything, anything you like Miss Mordecai. Just tell me...please say yes...some day you'll let me take you around the world. England, America, Japan, everywhere!"

She looked at him steadily, her blue eyes greyer. He repeated, "Please say yes." His eyes did not meet her gaze but slowly shifted to her chin, the mole, the neck, the thin silver chain, the mole.

"She will laugh at me now. I can't stand her. I want to put a knife through her cruel heart. I want to pour marmalade all over her from top to toe and make red ants eat her. She's so nasty, she will tell the entire class about this," Javed was sure. She didn't. Instead, she paused and said, "Come here, my boy..." She hugged him. Crying lightly, she purred, "That is the most beautiful gift anyone has ever given me. No one has gifted me a trip around the world. Go now...go...go...and don't fill your head up with such ideas. Some day you'll find a girl you will really truly love..."

She hugged him again. Instantly, Javed felt the silver chain on his face, her neck, the moles. Her slender arms encircled him for an eternity. He touched her hair. She wiped her soft tears away; she kissed him, her lips brushing his ears, his face, flying past his lips. No perhaps her lips did touch his.

The downpour ceased. The school bus arrived. Mr Dexter was waiting, *phatphati* gargling away on fuel monstrously. Javed left the staff room in a haze, the curtains swaying in a congratulatory jig. He was walking on sunflower-yellow clouds. Just for a moment, the rains returned.

Today he likes to think that the lips did rest on his—the kiss of an angel.

Time adds details—imagined, lived—to memories.

Today he would like to search for Miss Mordecai till the end of the earth and tell her that he never revealed her secret. Nor would she have revealed his. If she were still there, he would coax her to quit smoking. He would visit every city of the world with her, her alabaster arm in his. He would visit the art galleries with her to see Rembrandt, Van Gogh and Gauguin.

Before Javed swept her off to a world of beauty, Mr Dexter would be challenged to a duel. A coward, on the appointed day, Mr Dexter would leave town at the crack of dawn.

The child, boy, man would also tell Miss Mordecai that he never did find a girl whom he loved as much as her. And that he never found a girl who hugged him the way she did. Twice. On a wet, monsoon day with a sting of sunshine.

Anwari's Last Laugh

It was a CA: cardiac arrest. No need to panic. She's out of danger. She'll be shifted from the ICU to a private room tomorrow. Her lungs have packed up, yet there's no danger of her dropping dead-dead-DEAD. She'll be back on her feet, tightrope teetering. It's age; it'll happens to all of us. "In case you've forgotten, we all have got to go, sometimes before our time, way beyond our time," junior doctor commiserates on night duty at the newish Saifee Hospital, a Middle Eastern-style monolith right in the clogged belly of Charni Road. The junior doctor's phrases possess the phantom reverberation of a voice mail. Can't blame him, he's practising the prattle perfected by the seasoned.

Next morning, she was gone anyway, super dead. No tightrope, no teetering. Junior's seniors had tried. She's up there at heaven's wide open door. A queue there possibly but you know how it is...we all got to go.

How about a cup of tea in the cafeteria? Turn left from the hospital's door, then right, bang opposite the local railway station, actually closer to the overbridge and you'll find it. You can never get lost in Mumbai, least of all in a hospital.

Anwari Chaudhary's nephew, Sadiq Ali, didn't taste the tea-bag-tea from the ribbed paper cup. He was listening to junior doctor's chatter, as he would to elevator muzak.

"I'm not an intern," the wiry youngster said, as apologetic as the city's 8 a.m. faint, breezy January morning. "I'm a doctor. I turned 26 last month. Many responsibilities here. I attend to emergencies. That's why I was attending to your aunt...she's your aunt if I'm right. We put on her a mild form of ventilator, a DBD; she responded well. Then she died of COBC and CA, sudden."

DBD, COBC and CA...Sadiq didn't solicit elaboration. DBD ETC ETC fall through the cracks of his acronym-weary head. More natter, "In her case history, it is said she would smoke the hookah, she had quit...but hookah..."

DBD, COBC, CA. And hookah. Such evocative imagery, *mashallah. mashallah, nazar naa lage.* He visualised Aunt Anwari puffing away as regally as the miniatures of a Mughal-era empress. *Na, na,* she was never that cool. As a child, Sadiq had watched another woman, Begum Gulan, the second wife of Nawab Zayed Nur Jung, dangling a lazy hand for her after-meal hubble bubble. Infinitely classier than Anwari Chaudhary, some woman, that Begum Gulan. Her breasts musk melons, rounded, rising with every breath. He could watch them like films.

Quick intermission.

The breasts would descend, rise again to a climax. Don't reveal the ending.

Hyderabad's Begum Gulan had been lost in the bylanes of his memory. Today her painted-pink plump face morphed into Mumbai's Anwari's colourless bloated one, eyes shuttered on an ICU bed.

Gulan must be dead too. He had never thought of her till this hospital conversation, going all over the place, with the junior doctor. At the cafeteria, a Qatar sheikh's extended family prattled on about surgical procedures: the sheikh was being ripped open; an infection had to be controlled. He wasn't ready to knock on heaven's door, not yet.

Begum Gulan, Anwari, the nil-by-mouth status of the sheikh...the trio swirled in his head. He could feel his own heart hobbling inside.

Stop. Remember.

For his winter holidays, boy Sadiq would be dragged by his ears to the Bombay Central Railway Station. No Christmas with the Indian Santa Claus—cutely called Chacha Deepak, for him. No gully cricket with school friends, no *bhel puri* romps at Chowpatty. Just an overnight fretful train ride to Hyderabad.

He detested the family trip. It wasn't much of a family: his inscrutable parents, his mother's servile sister Anwari. She was the chaperone, *ayah,* a presence because the family could not deal with her absence. Poor Anwari poor, poor, she felt poorer than the urchins begging at the traffic light junctions. At least they smiled.

Anwari's sister smiled even in her sleep. She smiled while handing over her son, "Take him out for a walk, Anno *aapa*. He just loves to be with you," the decision was taken for him. He pulled out his tongue but was ignored; it would have become an issue.

Sadiq's parents shared a friendship of convenience with Nawab Zayed Nur Jung. Sadiq's father would genuflect before him, laugh uproariously at the Nawab's anecdotes about the British Raj and the Congress Party's struggle to coax royalty to cede to the Indian republic. Sadiq, still an adolescent, would catch the Nawab eyeing his mother while his father would serve himself one more continent-sized peg from the crystal whisky decanter. There must have been riotous sex: a group, a threesome, a foursome with Begum Gulan perhaps, a winter frolic from which Anwari was excluded, as a pariah would be from the fornication of the pedigreed.

She was nanny to him; she leashed the restless kid away from the adult *ménage à trois,* perhaps *à quatre. A cinq?*

The Nawab would show off his Impala in the mornings to Sadiq, and to Anwari who would look more unimpressed than an unlettered would with excellent prose. The Nawab's estate, encircled by forestland in the underdeveloped Hyderabad of the 1950s, would fall silent for clockwork siestas. Away in her *zenana* chamber, mid-afternoon, Begum Gulan would curse the Nawab's first wife Jahaan Bilqis Jung, who was more than outspoken about her enforced retirement from the royal bed, and who knows...bucolic experiments with the December guests from Bombay.

Begum Gulan would reason that Bilqis Jung had feasted sufficiently of her conjugal banquet. He had lavished attention on her for years, and look at her, just look at her. The *biryanis*, *kheer, tamatar saalans* and smoked *baingan saalan* did not show on the emaciated, official wife of the Nawab. Not that he was Eros in an *achkan*. He was unmanly, bisexual obviously. So what? Aberrations are secondary. Men are lords and masters, the penis gymnasts, the procreators. A woman must retire gracefully when she's not desired. Jahaan Bilqis was to smell the *kheer,* understand that she was expendable as a tray of *zarda*-laden *paans* after an evening. Begum Gulan was becoming rounder than a full moon. Edibly voluptuous. Eerieotic.

Stop this, Sadiq. Such wicked, chauvinistic cogitations. He was disrespecting his Aunt Anwari; he had just touched the *'ayah's'* face, bloated beyond recognition. It was colder in her room than the café's merciless air-conditioning. Also, why was he ping-ponging between Anwari and Begum Gulan, as unlike as black and white? Think grey.

The junior doctor sp-sp-spoke on. The bereaved Sadiq was in another world.

As a child, he was certain that Nawabs were superior men. They had the birthright to stray. Now in retrospect, he conjectured that the Nawab's first begum, Jahaan Bilqis, couldn't be sexually neutered. Come evening, she would be massaged with almond oil by her attendants. To spite the Nawab, she had two favourites of both gender. The Nawab was amused, some day he would join the three of them. Three, four, care not. His *rakhel* Begum Gulan could join him in richer, Bombay-imported pleasures, strip the winter guests who were like birds in transit.

The little boy heard robust male laughter, puppyish squeals, jazz and *ghazal*s alternate on the record player. Louis Armstrong, Nat King Cole, Iqbal Bano and Begum Akhtar re-re-played. Although the child and his unattractive *ayah* were lodged in the palace's remotest wing, the night breeze carried the sounds to the boy. He placed two pillows on his ear, grumbling, "It's so late. Why can't they go to sleep? Or let me sleep. I hate this."

Before and after those Hyderabad palace holidays, Anwari related ribald, half-imagined stories to a pre-adolescent Sadiq. She corrupted her nephew; she did not like him. He was the son of her younger sister, vivacious, a fashion plate, a seductress in satin *sharara*s, star-and-moon embroidered *dupatta*s, bee-stung lips. Men looked at her with lust; Anwari they either ignored or felt revulsed by her pockmarked face. She could have been presentable, were it not for that damned childhood chicken pox. She had scratched her face to craters.

Anwari was the second fiddle. Broken strings which played unpleasant music. She never spoke; she was afraid. Her voice was a pin scratching on vinyl, her neck and hands sallow. This Anwari blamed on her addiction to black tea. "If you drink too much *chai,* you darken," she told him.

"So why don't you drink milk?" the boy had asked.

"Shut up," Anwari had seethed. She could have slapped him across the face; she didn't. He would have ratted on her. Gutless, she avoided confrontations.

Junior doctor, the sheikh's loquacious sheikha, a faceless waiter thumping a bill in a metal saucer flecked by salted *saunf*...Sadiq gaped glumly at a plate of fried eggs turning ice-cold before the sheikha, her hand multi-tasking with prayer beads. No one in that hospital could have guessed that the fortyish man, Sadiq, was muffling a scream.

Stop, stop, STOP. A minute's silence please...at least.

No one mourns for the departed unless there's a personal stake. Anwari was his aunt, a woman who had lived and subsisted alone. Strangely she had amassed a fortune by sheer stealth and native intelligence. She deserved respect from the cafeteria. From Sadiq she deserved a hundred whispered recitations of the *kalima.* She wasn't about to receive any. Instead, she would receive a burial, the *kafan* and the rituals to be paid for from her own nest egg.

From the thin bunch of rupees doled out to her by her sister over the decades, Anwari Chaudhary had invested her savings in an apartment close to the city's notorious red-light precinct, Falkland Road, named after a British governor general. She rented out half her acquisition to a sex worker gone legit. By smart calculation, Anwari became the landlady of three more apartments, all rented out to women who had sought voluntary retirement from their trade.

The monthly rents Anwari invested in gold, shares and debentures. She was as independent as any hotshot businessman but lived frugally, surviving on rice, *daal* and *bhindi* fries. Half a *tandoori* chicken was nibbled only on special days—there weren't many. Content with her lifestyle, she informed her sister one fine day that blood was thinner than water. She would be an *ayah* no more, whipping out a 100-rupee note as a Ramzan Eidi for Sadiq. The boy looked at his mother for approval. She nodded. He took it and jabbed it in his *sherwani* pocket. "Enough, our *rishta* ends here. You have used me, I have cleaned your toilets, swept the floors. I had no choice. Today, I have a choice...and the choice is..."

"Don't say it, Anno...I always meant well," Sadiq's mother gasped.

"Meant well! Thank you for your kindness *aapa*. But I have to say it. From today I am dead for you and you are dead for me."

Her boney shoulders hunched, Anwari Chaudhary walked out of the small bungalow the Alis had made their home on Colaba Causeway, an address associated with old money. The nouveau riche were still struggling to reach that causeway. Sadiq's mother wept hysterically. The boy saw her as a movie heroine; in the 1950s, the black-and-white leading ladies cried so splendidly that they looked drop-dead beautiful. Fat shining tears flowed across the landscape of her cheeks. Really, his mother looked like a slighted angel when she cried. His father had to console her, "Anno is just doing drama...she'll be back."

She didn't return except at the *chaalisva* of Sadiq's parents. They were involved in a freak accident, a short circuit in the air-conditioning duct of an Udaipur Palace suite. The chamber was ablaze in a matter of minutes. Before they could escape their bodies were charred beyond recognition. They had arrived there to attend a *jashn* of Baul singers famous for their centuries-old folk music. An industrialist eager to social climb had heard of the beauty of Sadiq's mother, of her vivaciousness. She, with her husband almost as a tag-on, had been asked to stay on also for a tiger hunt the morning after the *jashn*. Her presence assured an ambience of sensuality and seduction.

No foul play was suspected. Their bodies were air-lifted to Mumbai, buried with the customary rites. On the fortieth day of their death by fire, the parents had to be remembered. A *faatiya* of *biryani* and *kheer* had to be blessed by the *mullah*s so that his parents' souls could rest in peace. RIP. Is that sourced from Rip Van Winkle, eternally asleep?

Sadiq looked on silently at the knotted rope of mourners at his sea-facing home. He cried because that was expected of him. Anwari Chaudhary arrived silently, left silently, shoving another 100-rupee note into his palm. Stupidly, he thought of buying a box of Luna colour pencils, illustrated with a boat and a half moon. Wonderful, he could own one now, sketch his mother smiling, and father smiling, smiling, smiling, smiling. He stopped crying.

Submitted to the guardianship of his father's parents in Hounslow, a colony for immigrant Indians and Pakistanis, Sadiq entered another realm. They secured his admission in a multi-cultural school, imparting Anglo-Saxon education. He spoke English more fluently than the Cockney Toms, Dicks and Harries.

Sadiq's father had eloped. His grandparents had not forgiven him. Devoutly religious, the orthodox pair sought solace in another belief: their son's death was the outcome of sacrilege. The boy reminded them of a son who hadn't obeyed, scripting himself a destiny that had to end in tragedy. So be it. His boy was here. They wouldn't allow his mother's family any rights to see him. He was under their charge, no intruders allowed. Aunt Anwari Chaudhary didn't exist in their holy book either. Let the boy get the best education which money could buy. The rest was up to destiny, whatever that convenient D-word means.

Sadiq must have been eight or nine at the time of the Udaipur conflagration—an age which later adulthood obfuscates. Yet, the memory of the *chaalisva* continues to rattle him.

Nawab Zayed Nur Jung did not attend. Neither did scarecrow Jahaan Bilqis Jung. If his memory serves him right, *rakhel* Gulan Begum did make a brief appearance, ruffled his hair, wept, *"O mere bache, mere bache, bache.* May Allah save you from the evil eye." Her melons pressing on him, her scarlet lipstick violated his white shirt collar. She left a *taweez* in his palm, whispering, "Keep it with you. It's our secret. It will prevent you from harm."

He still has that amulet, silver-plated, red-threaded, rusting among his childhood possessions preserved in a tin-box of biscuits. Glucose.

❧

The sheikha hissed over her ignored breakfast, "We should have taken him to London, this place is so... not right."

Junior doctor smiled, "How can she say that? We have the best facilities, best doctors, best..." His bests continued...medicines, hygiene, meals, nurses, interns, and...he added, fresh doctors like him eager to dedicate their lives to meagre pays and overtime, unremunerated service.

Sadiq wanted to rush out, pick up a pack of cigarettes from the vendor sitting before the beeping traffic in a nohorn zone. Anwari Chaudhary smoked a hookah; he had puffed at his first cigarette in Hounslow, the freckle-faced Brit kids, passing a weed around as if it were an invitation to a mind-trip. He had inhaled expertly, remembering the Hyderabad Nawab dangling a Du Maurier from his papyrus-thin lips.

Du Maurier cigarettes, elegantly arranged in a snappy platinum case, the Nawab would share them only with the boy's mother. Named after actor Gerald Du Maurier, the smokes spelt literary enticement. Gerald's daughter Daphne was the author of the legendary whodunit *Rebecca*. The platinum case, the murder mystery, these returned absurdly to Sadiq in that decaffeinated cafeteria. Aunt Anwari, he imagined, must have sneaked some from the case. Did she? He couldn't recollect. "Why the hell am I thinking of those damn smooth Du Mauriers?" He longed for a two-rupee Gold Flake to corrode his lungs at this moment.

Junior doctor repeated, a tinpot one-man-chorus, "Sir, don't look so depressed. It has to come to all of us...we have to go some time."

Mortality...forget those cigarettes.

Junior doctor had consoled Sadiq that his aunt was out of danger. She hadn't been. How dare he misinform? Sadiq could have punched his face. A breath away, the sheikha was about to feign a fainting fit. Actress, born natural. Sadiq wanted to leave; he couldn't. He had to express remorse.

Allah was watching. No forgiveness for walking away from a corpse.

The *kafan,* her last bath, her final ride to the cemetery, a five-minute drive away. Convenient, come to think of it, so many hospitals are located at a zip away to graveyards and crematoria. He must watch her being placed in an ambulance by professionals who do this every day. Don't they fucking care? How, just *how* can they remain unaffected?

Anwari Chaudhary, Jahaan Bilquis Jung, Begum Gulan tangoed around Sadiq. Invisibly in the cafeteria. They mocked him, preyed upon him. They stopped when junior doctor apologised—he had patients to attend to, they may live till tomorrow, maybe not. He offered his rose-petals-soft hand to Sadiq, who clasped it gratefully, relieved that junior doctor would leave him alone at long last. The sheikha and party he would delete—to do what he must. Pray a little prayer, the *kalima* in her memory. *"Laahe laaha illillah,"* he said to himself, *"Muhammad rasool illa..."* over and over again.

He walked on the unevenly tiled pavement. No, he wouldn't go to the Sonapur cemetery where she would be buried in a six-foot stretch next to his mother. That was her instruction. In a faded white envelope, she had left the money for her burial rites. No debt in death.

He didn't care. She had never liked him, she had been needlessly rough on him. She had concocted stories, that she had bathed him, first, when he was born. "Just get out of my life, now," he wished he could scream at her in that grave. "I don't want to think of you ever again. You never cared about me...you bloody..."

Shut up. The dead can hear. He halted at a red light which remained red for an eternity. His cell phone, forgotten in his breast pocket, rang.

Sadiq listened to a voice, crisp and expressionless, "Our deepest condolences."

"Thank you."

The voice continued. "I am Batliboi from Batliboi & Sons. We represent Anwari Chaudhary. We could not find you at the hospital."

"Tell me."

"I am Soli Batliboi, junior solicitor, representing her legal interests. We have to inform you...actually it might be better perhaps if you could drop in at our office. Fort, Yazdani Street...today 4 o'clock."

"I am not visting any lawyer's office. I am busy."

"So are we Sir, so are we...Tomorrow then...at 11 a.m."

"What is it?"

"We are executors of her will. She has left all her property and assets to you...did you not know this?"

Sadiq did not answer.

"All yours once we complete the probate formalities. Minus our professional fees, it's a good amount of money. We just need some signatures from you. Sir, many congratulations."

"I do not want her money."

Excuse me?

"What do we do with it?"

"I don't know...whatever you want."

"Sir...but."

"Forget it. I am not interested."

He switched off the cell phone. The traffic light was still red, perhaps a system failure.

Sadiq Ali didn't hear the train pulling into the railway station across the road, the way he didn't hear the junior doctor. He felt old and mortal for the first time in his life. Still at the traffic junction's red light, he cried, loud, very loud. Just couldn't stop.

And hasn't right to this day, to this very moment.

SHE IS LEAVING HOME

She was ready to go. Sona had just been dressed up ceremoniously in a silk sari. The temple priest applied a red *tika*, a powder flame to her forehead, and accepted ₹ 100, a paltry fee for the ritual. The currency note was better than nothing; this girl's wretched grandmother expected blessings for so little.

Granted. Fees are slashed for the poor. God will be happy happy happy.

The priest wouldn't have been charitable if she weren't leaving that day by the only bus which picked up passengers before sundown. Sona was leaving home; she had been sold to the commission agent from Mumbai's Dilruba brothel on Playhouse. The five-room brothel doubled by plywood partitions, specialised in virgins at a premium—₹ 1.25 lakh. The clients upwards of 50 years, new money sahibs propped on aphrodisiacs and made-in-Japan sprays, originated from the diamond brokering centre around the corner. Proximity is a plus. The mature can still be fetishist about virgins. In a similar vein,

Dilruba, 9 p.m.-9 a.m., prospered on flesh trade 24x7. No holidays, no sick leave.

After their 'deflowering' night, girls are retained at Dilruba till they command a clientele of six to seven men an evening. The event is spoken about with a finger pointed teasingly at the right nostril: the girl loses her *'nath'*—nose ring. On an average, a decade and half later the out-of-favour women become the establishment's cooks, cleaners, masseurs, rot like their teeth, and die before sprouting their first grey hair. If they have borne children, the sons and daughters perform the last rites. If not, a municipal van transports their bodies to a crematorium or burial ground on the specification of the madame in charge at the time. Every inmate of the brothel contributes towards the shroud and ritual expenses. There are tears, abstinence from meals for a day but not from the clients. Nothing changes in Mumbai's Dilruba; nothing changes for the girls sold to the brothel—controlled by a subterranean mafia—which specialises in virgins.

Flesh trade, what a world. Hurry, hurry, let the girl in the red sari and *tika* leave. She was born to be sold, rates not at all negotiable beyond a point. She is mute, uncomplaining. This is her destiny. Don't know what that means. It isn't tangible, it's an apology, a reproof. Forget it, she can't do a thing. Till her dying day, she will remember the priest. He has just sanctioned another life for her. Anything is better than lingering on in the wilds, circumambulating the temple rumoured to be more than five centuries old. No one wants her there, no one loves her. They couldn't have. They have just sold her so they—her family—could live, subsist.

If it wasn't Mumbai's Dilruba, GB Road's Mumtaz Palace was the next stop for the Jhalmora girls in this trade. If not Mumtaz Palace, there was Neelam Lodge of Chennai, discredited with dubious links to a three-storey Bangkok brothel notorious for its peripheral porn film production. No, no, it cannot come to that; the girl will remain in her own land. Men will enter her in a language she can comprehend; she will not be helpless. She will survive, she will get used to the savage thrusts and slaps. Any day better than starvation. Almost 12 now...she'll understand. She is leaving a collection of stones, tarpaulin, mud, somehow clapped together in Jhalmora, a freckle in a mountain state of north India. She is leaving home.

Twelve winters ago in Jhalmora, honeycombs had buzzed more busily than they do in the silhouetted forests just about visible from the temple. On the damp ground, a woman lay in labour but silent. Without a scream, the mother-to-be, Kishori, gave birth to a daughter. There was something significant about the child—so many of them in the honeycomb valley—it was a shade rosier complexioned, clearer-eyed, hands and feet already surely contoured. Can't distinguish infants from one another minutes after birth but this newborn was extraordinary. She didn't howl for her mother's breast. She smiled, her mouth a twitching crescent moon.

The white topped mountains looked on. It had snowed but the winds weren't furious that night. The girl was cocooned in an old cardigan and an embroidered cap. She gurgled, smiled, slept, made light sounds. Before her feeds, she moved her fingers like an orchestra conductor.

The newborn's grandmother, Mishta, was pleased. A daughter is an asset; she would do as she was told to; she would be sold on reaching puberty, the sooner the better. Mishta lit a palm-sized oil lamp to propitiate the gods. There was no money to buy the temple priest's blessing then. Kishori was half conscious. It was her first child. The labour pains had stabbed her insides. She couldn't scream; she couldn't cry. She had survived. Mothers must.

Cribbed in a rudimentary cotton-lined straw mat, the infant was just another transient addition to Jhalmora's beekeeping community. It belonged to the rugged, mountain valley surroundings, deceptively beautiful since the day of creation. At work on the open-air factory grounds, infants would be strapped to their mothers' stooping backs while they added apple extracts to the honey gathered by the men. Women sapped of energy left their infants on a carpet of green leaves, protected by patchwork cloth tents, just in case the Queen Bee in the nearby enclosure sought to revolt one fine morning.

Adults could be stung but for the infants a sting could be fatal.

Mishta, tough boned and broad framed, would not dream of any harm coming to the newborn. She tended to her at home, rocking her cloth cradle, singing off-key songs devoted to the mountain gods. A frog leapt in her throat but for the infant her croaks were pure music.

Some three months after childbirth, grandmother Mishta wore her red woollen cap, a tobacco-colour shawl preserved through generations and histrionically set a match to a cheroot of brown tobacco. She had decided unilaterally, "We shall call her Sona. She's as valuable as gold."

An amateur seamstress, Kishori was hobbling around in their sun-deprived room, looking for a pair of scissors. Weight regained after childbirth, she felt better physically except for that pronounced limp in her right foot. Gold? No, this daughter of hers was hers, her flesh and blood. The mother rejected the name. She'd think of something else.

The grandmother would have none of that. "Leave such matters to me, Kishori. For the first time in your life, you have done well. You have given me a granddaughter. A boy is silver but a girl is gold. She will fetch a good price when she turns from a child into a woman."

Kishori said impassively, "She will perform all the jobs that a boy does. We will not send her away. I will not sell her."

"We are not freaks to enjoy such luxury. Boy or girl, they all go away from us some day," Mishta sighed like all women did in the valley.

"I didn't."

Mishta's recriminations surfaced. "Do I have to remind you why you didn't go away? That's because no one would have you...you were born lame. Lame! God willed it so. Consider yourself fortunate that some man at least planted his seed in you."

"He'll come back to me," Kishori hoped bravely.

"He's a bloody swine. He needs a slut every day and gets one. I would have chopped his balls off if he had not given us Sona."

"Sometimes I wish I had been born normal, that I too had been sold like the other girls. I hate you mother."

Mishta chortled, jabbing the air with the stinking cheroot, "I said the same hate-hate dialogue to my mother. Enough now. No one would buy you because of your lousy foot. My mother didn't let me go because she was as foolish as you. Gave me away here...imagine here... to an apology of a man, old as the hills. Couldn't get it up most of the time. Left me with you...just like him...weak, useless. God's given me justice at last. Sona is special. She will bring us fortune. We will live without worrying about our next meal."

"I could run away with her."

"Your feet wouldn't take you very far."

"My feet can carry me to hell. I'd be happier there."

"Hell is where you are," Mishta snuffed out the cheroot, saving half for later, her face now a portrait of affection, "Sona, Sona, my little treasure. See, she's smiling at me. So unlike her mother...My Sonu is pretty and obedient. She'll understand that men don't have brains. They think from below their belts."

"Her father will return to me...you will see."

Grandmother Mishta rocked the child bundled in grimy woollens, sing-songing, "Close your eyes, close your eyes, pretty child, pretty child. We women can dream. Men can't even do that. The world may not know about your birth but I do. Your big mummy loves you, loves you. And when there is love between big mummy and pretty child, who needs the rest of the world?

By twilight Jhalmora's workforce of 35 beekeepers stored the canisters from the honeycombs and started their trek home. Akhilesh Narayan was the most striking of the lot. Also the most sullen. He was riled for being dumb since he wouldn't join in the *bhajan*s at the end of the day. Those devotional plaints had been sung since centuries by the tired to ward off evil, and the snakes which lingered in the thickets.

Amidst the *bhajans,* Sainath Kumar, his only friend in the group, nudged Akhilesh, "Missing your woman? Don't. There's plenty of honey everywhere."

Akhilesh did not respond. Sainath nudged him again, "Silence suggests sorrow. Cheer up." They broke off from the group to drink at a fireside camp where raw liquor was vended throughout the day. Akhilesh drank a potent extract of oranges mixed with spirit. Sainath kept pace, egging his friend on, "Liquor's our fuel like oil is for a lamp." And then another nudge, "Let's go and do whatever we must every night."

Akhilesh was hesitant. He gazed at the fire flames licking a black sky. He hadn't done badly for the day. He had many rivals but they never failed to acknowledge him as the best beekeeper of the valley.

Sainath said, "Forget that crippled woman. That child could be anyone's Akhilesh. She's got you by the short hair."

"Shut your mouth. Who cares!"

"I do. She's not a bad seamstress. During summer she earns a decent income."

Women waited at a clearing before the forests ended...a dozen women with the regular dozen customers. Akhilesh didn't utter a word to any of the women who inquired coyly, "You don't like us anymore or what?" Sainath pulled a woman roughly to him; Akhikesh walked away. Something was wrong with him, or perhaps for once, his instincts were right...he needed Kishori; he needed to be with their child. He imagined his daughter in his arms. Yet he vacillated. He was about to cross the stone hovel where grandmother Mishta was massaging her own legs with oil and grumbling, "Every winter is a trial, every winter. Sona doesn't seem to think so. How happily she's drawing milk from your breasts. Unlike her, you used to cry day and night for your feed. You were such a difficult child. Not like my Sona."

"She's not yours. I'll never part with her."

"We shall see," the grandmother retreated into a patchwork quilt.

❧

Akhilesh waited outside the stone house. He cracked five twigs consecutively, a signal he had used for Kishori in the past. She crept out in the dark, stood at a distance from his silhouette, and said reproachfully, "I suppose you have no need for me but we have a child. It's been three months but you have not come to see her."

Akhilesh had rehearsed what he would say to her, "I have no intention of seeing her. She could be anyone's."

Kishori shuddered in the dark, "You promised me that we would go away from here, to the city."

"Every man says that."

"I will not beg you then. Fuck a thousand women but you will never find another Kishori."

"I don't want you. Go your way but take this for her." He handed over a black lacquer box with a 50-rupee note in it. Uncharacteristically, his voice softened, "Please don't say no. Just take it."

Akhilesh walked on in the cold, hating himself. He wasn't the man he thought he was. He was afraid of responsibilities; he couldn't possibly bring a woman and child home. He had no home. He had lived alone all his life, always would.

In the stone hovel, grandmother Mishta flung the patchwork quilt aside, and muttered, "I can smell a man on you. I don't care who he is but did he pay you?"

Kishori handed over the lacquer box to her mother, then breast-fed Sona. Pocketing the 50-rupee note, Mishta gloated, "That's a windfall ...it'll see us through the rest of winter. I know who left it here for us. I was mistaken. No man would want to touch you. It must be a gift from Lord Ganesha. At the temple I had requested him to help us and look he has."

"Gods don't leave paper money, mother."

"Be grateful for his mercies. Lord Ganesha be praised."

On completing her first year, Sona was baptised traditionally by a temple priest. Intricate rituals were performed. A coconut was broken, conch shells blown, temple bells rung. Mishta distributed jaggery sweets among women who asked for more. They didn't get second helpings. "Be off, you witches. You are never there for us when we are in need," Mishta reminded them.

The temple priest intervened, "Mishta *mai* give with generosity, not with pride. And if I may say so, I wish you had named the child Durga, the Goddess of Power. Sona means little for us. What are we to do with gold and such material wealth?"

Mishta retorted, "Gold is not only material wealth, it is also spiritual wealth. It helps us to reach your gods and goddesses including Durga. The day Sona brings some more prosperity to our home, we shall remember you."

"So be it. Has the child's father not accepted her? Where is he?"

"We don't know," the grandmother retaliated. "Women must fend for themselves. If you are suggesting marriage vows between my daughter and the child's father, forget it. Vows break with more regularity than storms here. I did not go through the vows. Why should my daughter?"

The priest was offended. Kishori apologised, "She doesn't mean what she says."

Accustomed to slights, he said, "So be it. The gods see all; they know all. They will protect your child."

They didn't come to Akhilesh's rescue at the honeycombs that morning. His protective mask fell and he was stung by a swarm of bees. Flower paste was applied on his face. It was a bad omen.

A seasoned beekeeper intoned, "You must have done something to displease the gods."

Akhilesh would be given a reduced daily wage from now on. He would have to leave; he had been punished.

He would never be forgiven. He would never be the best beekeeper in his own eyes or of Jhalmora's.

Sainath handed over a battered wooden suitcase to Akhilesh, forcing him into a parting embrace. Akhilesh caught the next bus out; the golden girl's father would never return to the valley. Just as well for Sainath. He proposed to Kishori. The priest formalised their union. Grandmother Mishta disapproved the match vehemently, "What you have done is sinful. You're a whore. But I want to make it clear that he will have no rights over my grandchild."

Sainath said humbly, "My friend's child will be like mine. Akhilesh couldn't stay here anymore. The Queen Bee's sting is a curse. He has gone to the plains. Maybe he'll find some occupation, maybe not."

Mishta cried, "Let him rot."

The immediate future had been charted by Sainath: "Akhilesh has promised to send ₹ 50 for his child every month if he can. I will also contribute whatever I can to the house."

Mishta said tartly, "I am very capable of looking after myself, my daughter and grandchild. Now leave me alone with my Sonu."

Kishori handed over the infant but did say, "Mother, you don't affect me anymore."

"That's not a sign of your strength but a sign of your weakness. It's obvious that you cannot live without a man between your legs."

Mishta's judgement was final. It didn't make any difference to the newly- weds. Kishori and Sainath made love every night in the hovel. Mishta pretended not to hear her daughter moaning with pleasure.

Twelve years went by monotonously for the grandmother. She grew crankier, clocking the day till Sonu reached puberty. Sona's foster father, Sainath, was kind to her; he pampered her, occasionally fetching a yard of silk, glass bangles, kohl to highlight those coal black eyes. He favoured her over Nitin, the son born to Kishori a year after their marriage. Sona would pluck wild flowers for her Sainath *papa,* once bringing home a snake on a stick as a gift. Grandmother Mishta had been horrified. Snakes were saintly, not to be trifled with. The girl doted on her brother, Nitin, treating him more preciously than a thousand pearls.

The self-exiled beekeeper, Akhilesh, did not maintain any contact but the postman would unfailingly deliver a money order of ₹ 50 every month. The sum should have increased; it didn't. Grandmother Mishta would snatch the money from the postman, praising Lord Ganesha "who continues to shower his mercy upon us."

Mothers in Jhalmora had trained their children to beg in the marketplace every morning. All the community's children were proud to beg; they contributed to their upkeep ever since they could walk. Kishori and Sainath earned their wages, while the ₹ 50 would initially be stored in the lacquer box as a mark of reverence to Lord Ganesha, then spent on the old woman's medicines.

~

The commission agent from Dilruba was on his shopping trip. Sona was quite easily the catch of the annual crop. A perfect set of teeth; eyes radiating innocence. She was neither petite nor large. Her hair fell in ripples over her shoulders. Her feet and hands were checked, and her grandmother vouched for her virginity, "I have been protecting her from the day she was born. Forget any man, I haven't permitted even strong gusts of wind to touch her, summer or winter."

The beekeeping business was in a slump that summer. Disease had broken out in Jhalmora's beehives. It was rumoured that the Queen Bee was annoyed with the valley. In the event, Sainath had been laid off. Kishori's services as a seamstress were no longer needed by women in the valley. Their son needed surgery for his inflamed tonsils. Sona had come of age at the opportune time. The girl was pleased that she would be of some use to her family, especially her grandmother. She'd had enough of Jhalmora, the valleys, the extremities of seasons: the winter hugs and sunshine caresses. Her ears had tired of the hum of the honeycombs; she could not identify a

Queen Bee; she did not believe that the illnesses, accidents and deaths in the valley stemmed from the wrath of the Queen Bee.

After a journey in a beautiful train, Sona would see a wonderful city of gold...like her name. She would see cars, tall-tall homes. She would eat ice-cream, and she would stand before an ocean, her toes tickling the sand. She would fold her hands before the sun; she would kneel before Surya *devta;* she would kiss the first love of her life...he would kiss her again, again...he would make her a woman. Sona so wanted to be a woman.

She wasn't naïve. She had heard thousands of stories of the big bad city. But she would be treated differently just the way she had been in the valley—special. She would be in the arms of a man; she would be her mother in the arms of Sainath *papa.* She would look for her real father, the man who sent ₹ 50 every month. She would cry when they met, "*Papa,* why did you go? Just because of those bees?" It wouldn't be easy but she would find him. Lord Ganesha would guide her. She would see her first movie; she would be fancy. She would wear better saris than the red one she was wearing right now. She would get a pair of jeans, dark glasses, pink and purple lipstick...

Sona, her face and smile covered under the sari's *pallu,* was being seen off at the Jhalmora bus terminal. The commission agent had paid the entire sum of money, with the proviso, "If she misbehaves, we send her right back. Immediate refund." That no girl bought by him could misbehave or was sent back was another story. Sona, blessed by the priest, couldn't possibly disobey. All her life she had been taught to obey.

At the bus terminal, her foster father clung on to Sona and wept, "Think well of us child, it is not our fault."

Her brother held on to her, "Sona *didi,* don't leave me alone."

Kishori, her mother, cried, "We women cannot write our destinies."

And grandmother Mishta kissed her Sona for the last time, her eyes aflame, "Sona, you are beautiful. You will be protected by Lord Ganesha wherever you go. Now sit in the bus quietly."

Sona glowed, "*Nani,* anything else?"

That's when grandmother Mishta broke down, shedding her first tears in 12 years, "Child, don't look back. Never, never look back. Go. Just go."

THE BALLIMARAN SISTERS

Knifing its way through Chandni Chowk, Ballimaran isn't a memory lane. Nazneen doesn't associate it with nostalgia at all. That would be as facile as reading a book merely for its time-tinted pages. She's resolute she will not tap into her yesterdays to silk-line her todays. She isn't distressed. She has to face a situation: it could be a crisis, a false alarm. She has to deal with it. She will. No use crying over spilt emotions. It was circumstantial, don't feel guilty...it'll all work out. Just be, Nazneen, just be.

On a ferociously hot October noon, her taxi lumbers past the Red Fort looking paternally over the Purani Dilliscape. She hasn't crossed the Phunwara junction, the Sis Gunj Gurdwara and the mouth leading to Paranthewalli Gali for close to a decade. Sons and daughters of the generation she had seen as a child look just like their elders once did—the same striped shirts, the same cola colour saris and the same hurried strides. Would be odd if crude macho abuses no longer polluted the air. She is not there for nostalgia. No homesickness either. The lane was never her home.

Ballimaran, the heart of Delhi 6, is a poem which cannot be written. Bifurcating into lanes capriciously, it is a blank verse, its metre and cadences beyond grammar. What's she making all this ado about? It's just another lane which lends itself to those-were-the-days flashbacks. Facetious, so facetious. To think that the present is tense because the past was so perfect. No difference between the now and then.

To strike a balance between romanticising and disparaging Ballimaran, Nazneen sees the tangible side of the lane: the clamour and the dirt. She associates the lane with murderous traffic, industrious faces which belong to another century, chisellers and cons, crushing poverty, mercantile optimism and the overpowering waft of saffron-flavoured *Changezi biryani.* The cab crawls past the scores of 'goggle' shops and vendors exchanging yards of silk for a pittance—did they steal the pink paisley swathes? Women bob through the manic melee in *burqa*s blacker than the kohl in their scarcely visible eyes. The cycle *rickshawalla*s' muscles are sculpted out of necessity, not vanity. And no status update on the opiated fruit vendors tucking into sliced guavas when business is slack, which it always is. Not surprising.

Imagine honking through the choked Ballimaran artery. Nerve-jangling. She pays off the cabby before the drama intensifies. The cabby heads out of the space-crunched *mohalla.* No point waiting for fares out here. They'll be for short, fuel-gobbling distances.

An overnight travel bag slung over her shoulder, Nazneen drifts into the long and winding stretch of flotsam. Textile shops starve for customers, pariah dogs gape drowsily as if drugged, and no one's bargaining with the ancient hawker wearing a dozen *faux* Burberry kitchen aprons on his lean frame. *Pachaas ke do, pachaas ke do.*

Mirza Ghalib's 18th century *haveli* during his last nine years is about the only barren courtyard in this world of assortments. Nazneen ducks tentatively into the heritage protected site on Gali Qasim Jaan. The poet's memory is preserved with no more than an uninspiring gallery, a verandah and a courtyard. Stray plaques, some calligraphy, scant mementoes. She should have studied Urdu. Regretfully, she cannot read the poetic lines inscribed on a plaque. Intuitively, the cell phone camera is focused on it, cool *click*. Someone will read it for her, and translate. Career-centric Mumbai didn't permit her the luxury of studying classical music, painting a violent symphony of colours on canvas or keeping publishable notes in a diary. *Get a job, get a higher pay packet, get a higher designation, get higher authority, get, get, get.* Initially, she wanted to scale the heights to win her parents' and sister's approval and accolades.

Nazneen Ikhlaque Ahmedboy and Ghazala Nisaar Qureshi were sisters by birth, but separated because their parents gave one away in adoption. Nazneen, the younger one, was 'gifted' to her childless maternal aunt in Mumbai. No family secret, that. In the 1960s and '70s, parents parting with a child so that it could have a more privileged future wasn't a once-in-a-blue-moon phenomenon. Five-year-old Ghazala, insanely fond of the new arrival, had been told that the warm pink bundle would be leaving their house but would visit every winter. She should be happy that her light-eyed, cherubic Nazneen, would receive more love, care and material comforts in her Mumbai home. Ghazala had brightened up, "Really? Then she must go. But I will see her again... won't I?"

The winter holiday pact was followed religiously. Nazneen's biological parents, the Qureshis, and *badi aapa* Ghazala treated her as if she were a Botticelli angel visiting their one-storey, crumbling home. It didn't have the amenities which the child was accustomed to at her foster parents' high-ceilinged bungalow on Bandra's Carter Road. No cars, Barbie dolls or fizzies and chocolates in the refrigerator. To compensate, her Delhi parents would pamper her silly with hugs and kisses. Ghazala didn't notice the favouritism. She would snuggle up in bed with Nazneen, her Naazo, who would be snatched away in a week. Big sister counted the days, praying that somehow she would be wrong in her calculations. Just two days left? Not fair! Allah, make it four...if not, at least three.

Right till her adolescence, Nazneen would be retrieved by the Ahmedboys at *the* appointed hour. The sisters would weep at the Paharganj Railway Station, deriving some consolation from their habit of writing letters to each other every Sunday. Ghazala would write four to five pages. Nazneen's reply would be on a single sheet of paper cleared by her foster parents. The adopted child was discouraged from complaining about trivialities like an upset stomach, her school homework becoming more punishing by the day or the same Sultana pudding served at home for dessert for a week.

Through school and college, Ghazala had remained rooted. She didn't budge from Kucha Rahman, yet another lane bifurcating from Ballimaran. Its aged wooden door with rusting iron-fittings are still there. Nothing should change for Nazneen, the past is misty, sepia shaded.

Nazneen hasn't been to Purani Dilli for years, and if truth be told, it's because she didn't want to. She avoids confrontations; she avoids situations which cannot be solved. She's no firefighter. Ghazala gave her limitless affection, but all these years Nazneen has been self-absorbed. It's too late to study Urdu, it is also too late to pretend that there is no distance between *badi aapa* and her darling Naazo. Force of circumstances.

Today, at 25, Nazneen can do nothing for Ghazala who has long been under treatment. Bi-weekly consultations with her psychiatrist, a daily mound of pills and round-the-clock vigilance are a must. Ghazala is not schizophrenic but she does conduct these silent conversations with herself. She doesn't suffer from depression, or loneliness. She prays five times a day, maintains all the *roza*s during the Ramazan month, and teaches *mohalla* children to read the Koran. In fact, Ballimaran's inhabitants are in awe of Ghazala *baaji.* They don't mind at all if she flies off the handle once in a while, cursing the invisible devil around her. "I will finish you *shaitaan.* Don't defy me, I will finish you," she screams, jabbing the air with an imaginary meat chopper. The neighbourhood children, *abba* Nisaar Qureshi and loyal family cook Yusuf *chacha,* attest that the devil has been vanquished, that she has succeeded in killing him. Well done! "If he dares to show his hideous face ever again, I will kill him again...and again," the seething Ghazala is embraced by her *abba.* He calls up her physician Dr DG Gupta. No she hasn't inflicted any injury on herself or on others. She has been given the emergency yellow-black pills. She is resting. "Very well. Keep me informed. You have my mobile number," the physician hangs up.

The scene has been played out many times over, without any improvement. *Bade abba* can't take it anymore. Without specifying the reason, he asks Nazneen's foster parents to allow her to come *home* as soon as possible. Not a request, a demand. Two days later, Nazneen had caught a flight to Delhi. Demand or request, she could not leave right away. Too much unfinished work at office, a presentation had to be readied at the international publishing house which had lately set up a branch in Mumbai. She edited manuscripts alternately boring and exhilarating. Secretly, she had begun work on her first novel, blending fact and fiction but hadn't gone beyond the first page of the first chapter. And now this summons.

The ground floor of the Qureshi home was leased out to carpet dealers from Kashmir. Nazneen climbed the narrow stone staircase, suddenly apprehensive. *Bade abba* hadn't fetched her from the airport, a signal that she wouldn't be treated like a princess entering a castle today. She could smell his *bidi. How will she hug him? Can't stand the stench.* Taking a deep breath, she walked straight up to him and embraced him before he could get up from his charpoy. "*Salaam alaikum bade abba,* you must stop smoking. It's not good for you," she pouted to which he retaliated, "But who wants to live?" Nazneen ignored his remark, and noticed that the two rooms facing her father's were empty. Yusuf *chacha* had taken Ghazala out to the bazaar; she wanted to cook *shaami kabab, shalgams* and *shakarkandi* for her Naazo.

"Really? How come I didn't see them in the lane?" muttered Nazneen.

"Do you see anything beyond your nose...Naazo?" *bade abba*'s words landed on her face like a slap. Spoiling for a fight, is he? She wasn't going to give him one. *Bade abba* lit another *bidi.* His daughter placed her travel bag on the fraying carpet, and settled on a *mudha* at his feet.

She had been taught to use reason instead of anger on being provoked, "I can understand that you are concerned about Ghazala. So am I but it's not fair to...how do I say it?...look at me as if I am guilty. I haven't done a thing which could harm her. I am not responsible for her state... you know that."

"You would like to believe that, wouldn't you, Naazo? Anyway, you must be tired after your flight. I'll make you some tea. Or would you like something cold?" he said, switching on the cooler under the only window in the despondent room.

"I'll help myself *bade abba*. Or have I become a stranger here?"

Bordering on the acrimonious, their conversation threatened to turn ugly. Nazneen retreated, touching her father's cheek, "You look so handsome in your stubble *bade abba*...but it hides your cleft chin." Her father softened, showed her to the guest room unoccupied since years, and before leaving, caught her hands in his, "I don't know what's right and what's wrong any more. Both of you are grown-up women...no longer babies...help me get our Ghazala back. Only you can...and yes, I will say, I am upset with you because you haven't returned her love. Never. She has been unlucky in love from her parents, from you...and from...it's all His will. *Parvardigar* gave too much to one and nothing to the other."

"Is that my fault?" Nazneen shot back bitterly as she closed the door on her father.

An hour and a shower later, she was ready to meet her Ballimaran sister. Ghazala was in the kitchen, stirring the *shalgam* stew. On hearing the guest room door open, she hurried towards Nazneen and hugged her hard and long till Nazneen felt smothered, "Do you want to kill me with your love, *aapa*?"

Yusuf *chacha* remarked, "How wonderful they look, *mashallah*." *Bade abba* smiled but with some effort. After *meetha paan*, the father retired, hoping the sisters would talk through the night but Ghazala excused herself. She was tired, she needed to catch some sleep right away.

Nazneen abandoned the crime thriller she had picked up at the airport. Same old Americans saving the world from extinction; same old Russians plotting the world's extinction. She switched off the bedside lamp but couldn't sleep. That old problem of new beds, new pillows... but come on, she had slept on this carved wooden bed through so many winter holidays; it hadn't changed. Kucha Rahman was silent, exhausted. If it were Mumbai, perhaps she could have stood by the window and gazed at the sea. Not here. The home overlooked a dozen others, separated by a palm's distance. She was sweating. The cooler wasn't helping any. Neither was the suspicion that Ghazala had been pointedly aloof. After that magnum embrace, she hadn't asked Nazneen about her work, or her fiancé, Sohail Khatib, a high-flying multinational executive, whom she was to marry next year.

Life was good. Sohail and she sms'ed each other morning, day and night. Nazneen wasn't about to complicate her life. *Aapa* has a clinical disorder, right. She'd get over it *inshallah.* Everyone goes through heartache, emotional holocausts. Ghazala's disappointments had been severe but she could have dealt with them. Many women have endured worse; *aapa* proved to be weaker than she looked. Nazneen empathised with her but why had *bade abba* summoned her urgently? She was no miracle worker. He was aware that she talked with Ghazala over the phone every weekend. They exchanged emails. Their bond was steadfast but she couldn't do much more. Could she? She couldn't rewrite Ghazala's story or find another Anirudh Kapur whom she had loved deeply.

In the same theatre group of Nizamiya College, Anirudh and Ghazala had planned to marry secretly if their different religions came in the way. Before the parents could be approached, Ghazala was pregnant. Anirudh did not want to be a father so soon; he had to get a job, earn a livelihood. When she recoiled at the very idea of an abortion, he took the regular escape route of cowards—just disappeared from the city. Ghazala panicked, told her *abba* and *ammi* all. A clandestine abortion by a midwife at the Kucha Rahman house was *abba's* idea of avoiding shame and scandal. The abortion was a disaster. Ghazala bled profusely and had to be rushed to hospital where the physicians declared that if they were to save her, she would not bear a child...ever again.

Ghazala wasn't lynched by a mob at the Kucha Rahman *mohalla*. *Abba* and *ammi* said nothing, and for Nazneen it was a regular day in Mumbai. The whispers died a natural death. After all, Ghazala was such a delicate young woman, helpful to all, respectful to the elders and chummy with the children. The incident was forgotten by all...except Ghazala herself.

Seven years on, Ghazala continued to be hard on herself. She would neither talk about it to her psychiatrist, nor to anyone else at home. "She has to speak, do you understand that?" *bade abba* told Nazneen the next morning, while Ghazala extracted pomegranate juice in the kitchen for her Naazo. "I know she will speak to no one but you. Is that too much to ask of you? Speak to her if you still have regard for your real family...yes real...I am saying that today. We are your blood, not those fools who gave you all the comforts of the world...but not love."

Bade abba was right to an extent. Again Nazneen reasoned, "I know what you are saying is in anger. I did not ask to be adopted. You gave me away. As for speaking to Ghazala to make her open up—do you really think it's as simple as that? She will speak only when she wants to and to whom she wants to *if* she speaks at all."

The breakfast of *tandoor naans*, omelettes, milk and juice was ready on the *dastarkhan*. Had it been winter, *nihari* and *bevdiyan* would have been served to the daughter from Mumbai. The conversation between *bade abba* and Nazneen halted so abruptly that Ghazala asked,

"What! Are you both in mourning? You guys must either be remembering *ammi*...the lord preserve her in heaven... or saying rude things about me. Not fair!"

"Nothing of the sort *aapa*," Nazneen said gently. "*Achha* tell me *aapa*, how about a walk to the municipal park today before the sun gets really hot?"

Ghazala understood that her Naazo was trying to revive memories of their hide-and-seek games and gabbing about in that park. She declined politely, "There is nothing left there, Naazo. Now don't say you want to go to my old *madrassa*, the *gottiwalla* lemon, soda*walla*, Moti Talkies for a matinee show. We've done all that. Connaught Place, Jantar Mantar, India Gate...Qutb Minar...seen all that with you. What's the point of getting nostalgic? Nostalgia is no cure.We can't bring back the past my dear Naazo."

Nazneen fell silent. Their father sauntered off, pretending to search for his bundle of *bidi*s. Ghazala cleared the *dastarkhan*, and said cheerily that she wouldn't mind a walk to Mirza Ghalib's *haveli*. The sisters had never been there together.

"Strange you should suggest that *aapa*," Nazneen said. "Yesterday on my way, I had stopped in there for a minute."

"So would you like to spend some time there? I'd love to...but there's one problem. Yusuf *chacha* will have to cook lunch alone."

Bade abba did not hide the fact that he had been eavesdropping, "Ghazala...go ahead. I'll send Yusuf to get us *pasandas* and *gosht ka saalan* from Karim's. *Kababs* also. Or should I get Chinese?"

"Karim's! Karim's! Karim's!" the sisters yodelled in unison, delighted at their timing.

❧

The outing to Ghalib's *haveli* was spiritless. The sisters regretted the token acknowledgement to the poet. Bureaucratic apathy, they concluded. As much a tribute to a master poet as a wreath of plastic flowers. Nazneen googled a quote by the poet on her cell phone: *"I sleep in the courtyard. Two men carry me on to the verandah and dump me in a small, dark, side room. I attend the day lying in its dingy corner. I'm again carried out and dumped on the cot."*

Ghazala didn't find that pithy or poignant. "It's just another phase most of us have to go through...like *ammi* did. And I didn't tell you this before but when *ammi* went away, she did say something. You may not like this but she said I do want my Naazo here but that is not to be. Allah has willed it so. Don't call her. Ghazala, you're my only daughter."

Nazneen felt as though she had been whipped in Ghalib's *haveli*.

By evening, she planned to leave Delhi the next morning. *Bade abba*'s eyes welled over with silent allegations. Yusuf *chacha* pretended to be unaware of the crossfire of feelings. And Ghazala was behaving like a tragedy queen. Who needs this? They were being unbearably harsh on her. None of them asked her to extend her visit by a day, a couple of days. There was a time when they wouldn't let her leave, imploring her to stay on for another week at least. Nazneen tried to bring back the old times once again—a walk to the municipal park would be great. That's the spot where she had recited an imaginary story, a school essay—*Trip to the Moon*—to her *badi aapa*. The story was about a little girl on a silver rocket who had parachuted into a world of ice-cream, rainbow flowers, with a galaxy of princes competing for her attention. She had rejected all the princes and was leaving for her chamber, when she saw her dream prince's reflection in the moon. She had transported *aapa* to another world. *Aapa* had applauded at the end of the narration. *That* had encouraged Nazneen to write. She would post her school essays to *aapa,* sundry musings about happiness, anger, friendship and family ties. Eleven on ten from *aapa* each time. Without fail.

Nazneen pleaded, "*Aapa,* that's my only wish on this trip. Let's go back to the bench where you heard my story..."

"Trip to the Moon?"

"You remember? Please *aapa,* let's remember those days...before I return."

The sisters began their walk towards Chandni Chowk's mid-point, jostled and pushed by the sadistic surge of traffic. The park was still a distance away. Suddenly, Ghazala caught her sister's hand, "Suppose you... *Allah chaahe*...have a wonderful husband, a wonderful marriage...and two wonderful daughters, tell me...would you give one to me?"

In an instant Nazneen's face hardened into a death mask. Then all too visibly—before doubt settled on her face—she softened, and lied, "Of course I would give my daughter to you, *aapa*. You are my life. And just you wait, I will do just that."

They walked at a faster pace, arm-in-arm, towards the park.

And Ghazala *aapa* chirped happily, "You're my little little doll."

SCHEHEREZADE'S TEACUP

The cup, thick, pocked, porcelain bubbled, from a factory-produced set of 12—picked up from Iran's Isfahan flea market—was once packed in a carton lined with dead straw. Today it sat inertly, the shade of a camel's tooth, stained with rivers of ginger tea. The cup wasn't chipped; it couldn't be. It was hers, more treasured than her gold wedding band too loose now for any of her talons.

Her cup of *chai* was empty that sweltering Sunday, waiting to be filled at the fourth hour. Her waltzing eyes were accustomed to the curtained light which the going-blind negotiate with every morning. She would empty half the brew from a dented black tin bowl removed with a rag from the gas stove. The stove's knob would be flicked off quickly so there was no danger of explosion. The blue flame would fire a shot of red, vanishing into the partly coagulated perforations of the stove. Sugar stirred to the last grain, she liked the tea sweet, not too much, not too little.

The cup was her companion. She talked to it, wondering whether it was more comfortable on the marble-top table or on the olive-green stone floor. "Silly girl, be glad that you're still with me. You are old, you are precious. I am older but not precious," she goosed today even as the city outside at Dhobi Talao, a section of old Bombay overrun by buses, cars, scooters and bicycles, waited to clear its throat, rasp and cough. She hadn't ever named the cup, now it was too late for the christening. Cuppy, Cuppdi, Cupsoo, *chhaa* atrocious.

That Sunday the cup was to break, leaving behind a saucer, orphaned. Gogoosh, the fat vanilla-white cat, leapt on the marble top, unaware that she had just ended a love story between her mistress, Scheherezade Khushmandi, and the *chai* cup. Scheherezade turned sharply; a needle thin cry. Her heart leapt a fraction, resettled surprisingly swiftly, with that resigned nod of the head, acknowledging that all dependable things must perish some day. She picked up the pieces, thinking absurdly of a woman's body, bones, demolished in a car crash. She stooped, collected the cup's unharmed saucer lovingly but then chucked it away from the fourth-four balcony. The cup's shards followed, to be forgotten, never forgiven. She paused to hear the sound of porcelain hitting the road, baffled that her eyes hadn't moistened. "Maybe I've just seen too much. Nothing affects me any more," she babbled. "Who will I talk to? Gogoosh is flighty, unreliable. Really, who do these cats think they are? They think they have nine lives. Dirty *biladis*. One life is enough for all of us, especially cats. Gogoosh most of all. Just look at her, look at her, behaving as if she doesn't know she's broken my cup... my heart."

Scheherezade hoisted herself on to her high four-poster bed, its carved wavy spindles relieved by embossed ceramic tiles of a lurid blue waterfall, an angry sunset and a peach-complexioned flamingo. The bed monopolised the widow's room which barely had space to spare for a mirrored almirah, a nylon-cane chair of wrought iron legs, and a plank holding a portrait of Zoroaster alit by a stubby candle. Equal status was apportioned to a portrait, no bigger than a postcard, of Scheherezade's long-departed husband, Rustam Khushmandi, whose salient feature was a moustache the shape of Hitler's and as dense as Stalin's. She glanced wanly at the dead dodo, *aapro* Rustam, from the bed, as if to berate him for not offering condolences for the smashed cup, her *jaan*, her reason to feel secure in a room leading to a balcony. The day's laundry hung there every day, dripping water on the stone floor till the amoebic puddle was dried by the vigilante sun.

She swore churlishly to abstain from tea this Sunday, her private ceremony to mourn the death of a cup. She would not feed Gogoosh the breakfast *katora* of milk either; she would punish her some more by avoiding eye contact. Stupid fat cat, once a skinny ball of scabs and wounds. The creature had been picked up from the Tardeo traffic junction three years ago. "This is the way she shows her gratitude," Scheherezade moaned.

"I should have let her be eaten up by dogs, this horrible, *taddan gheli* Gogoosh."

Gogoosh paced around idly. Her mistress wrapped a coarse *chudder* over herself, muttering a prayer to Zoroaster, "*Khodaiji,* you've snatched away my cup of happiness. Give me courage to bear my loss." The prayer conducted, Scheherezade addressed the flamingo tile, "Look at this cat, just look at her." And to think Gogoosh was named after a popular Iranian singer who had left Khomeini's Tehran in exile; the songstress was considered decadently modern, a wanton woman. Gogoosh songs were about love, longing and seduction. Scheherezade had heard of her; she hadn't heard any of her songs. When the cat had to be named, she picked Gogoosh since it had a tongue-twisting musical ring to it. So, so unlike the tinny clatter she heard wafting from the radio...FM nowadays, no more Radio Ceylon. And whatever happened to the signature tune of Akashwani? Neighbours would switch on those transistor radio boxes as soon as the delivery boy, in Quink ink blue uniform from the Parsi Dairy Farm, left a dubiously measured *seer* of milk in a *tapeli* at the doorstep.

"*Khodaiji,* let everyone die, let me die...78 or is it 84? isn't an inauspicious age to go...or at least let me remain forever on this lousy bed, so many bugs, don't want to see them, let them suck my blood," the bereaved woman muttered. "Let me see if anyone cares. Let me see if my sons...sons...are men or farting donkeys?"

After an eternity of waking up at the break of every morning, she shuttered her eyes today, but wait there was something poking the pulp walls behind the eyelids. Cataracts they must be. She'll live with them, she'll die with them, thin they are, but acting up like mutinous soldiers. Maybe if she sobbed, the eyes wouldn't hurt. Maybe. Why should she sob? "Just sleep Scheherezade, sleep. Those donkeys-monkeys, my sons...imagine my sons!...can't get up to fill up the barrels and buckets in the kitchen with water. This municipal water service, no improvement, no improvement. For just half an hour they give us water, as if they are doing us a favour. Water isn't their father's property. I have a good mind to go and tell them *that* some day. The taps will run dry in another 15 minutes but ask me if I care?" she giggled with girlish pleasure.

She did care. She flung the *chudder* off her hunchbacked body, turned on the taps, aimed the mouths of rubber pipes into the barrels. Water splashed over from the barrels, the plastic buckets and the *tapelis* for the day's cooking. The part-time Gangabai would rustle up the routine Sunday lunch of lamb cutlets, French beans, *chapattis*. Scheherezade shuffled back to the room where Gogoosh circulated, unperturbed by her mistress who sat on the nylon-cane chair, finding herself useless. Sparrow-like she winged over again to the balcony, the street still on the cusp of morning hysteria. All that noise-noise, people walking-talking fast-fast, they should slow down, nothing is gained from going fast-fast every day, least of all on Sundays.

Days, what days Scheherezade? Wasn't it strange that she was still up and about despite witnessing so many births, accidents and deaths? Stop whining, not nice. She shuddered at the thought of priests in ageing pajamas and shirts entering the brown-stone agiary below. They seemed so content, so cool. What if they sensed her ingratitude to her lord?

"Don't get me wrong," she entreated the god who dwelt in the fire temple. "*Shun karu* boss! You have written a bad *kismat* for me; you should have given me finer criss-crosses on my palms." The fortune lines on her palms were splintered, incomplete, a warning that it wouldn't be a smooth ride. Naturally the cup had to break, one more piece of her had to shatter. "O Gogoosh," she carromed between remorse and revenge. "I should strangle you but I won't be able to stand your gasp before your neck is snapped. I won't be able to chuck your corpse into the gutter. Gogoosh, I want to punish you but can't do it. Thank *Khodaiji* for mercy. I'm a kind woman. No one has ever told me that, the stupids! No compliments, no appreciation. All stupids!"

The balcony was no solace. Ants—damn *moongis*—swarmed out of the ancient teakwood railing which exuded the scent of maroon cream pastry. She had hogged a pastry there, a jam cream puff too, last afternoon, crumbs forgotten. Scheherezade felt she would either cry or faint out of uncertainty, her feelings as tangled as a badly-knit sweater. Her youngest sons Jamshed and Mehernosh, middle aged, slept in the adjoining rooms, a room for each. Think they are bloody Lord Falklands. British Raj left, Indian government should also leave. Scheherezade will look after herself, thank you very much. Two sons had stayed, wallowing in bachelordom. The eldest of her brood had packed their bags, left the city, married, discarding her like childhood combs, shoes and caps. Cyrus was in Ontario, Canada; Danesh in New Jersey, America...both married to pale-skinned women. They must be fornicating with other women too. Men do that, her sons could not be exceptions to the machismo rite. Wives' bodies run dry of secrets. Men remain unaware that their wives are as tired of them as much as they are. Cyrus and Jamshed, go ahead, do as the Canadian and American adulterous fuckers do.

Adultery is like changing toothpaste brands. No difference in Mumbai, except that Jamshed and Mehernosh don't qualify for adultery. Must be visiting prostitutes at Colaba. They aren't saints, they need sex. Tanking up on cheap whisky, then taking off their vests for an hour or less of physical gratification...such sexy-vexy thoughts, *java de*, let it be, let the *ghelchodiya*s be.

Who cares?

Here she was suffering, struggling with electric currents zapping her head. The two bachelor sons were sleeping, dreaming who knows what. They couldn't hear her silent screams; they were born with ears immune to her protests, anyone's protests except their own.

No one ever heard her screams. That was Scheherezade's lifelong regret. Yet the very screams had kept her alive. No one had heard her when she was born either. The winds lashing the Yazd hill slopes were louder than her wails. Perhaps she had concocted the story, "I spin yarns. I don't know how I came into this world, what the exact year was, the date, what the place was." Revelling in memory blanks, she surmised that she was born in an orchard of sour limes. She was a matchstick of an infant, who went on to behave sulphurously through her childhood. Her only brother Bairam, younger by a single Navroz, was favoured by their mother, Rukhsin, a stout woman with an alabaster complexion and grey-blue eyes. The only benediction that Rukhsin had showered upon Scheherezade was her name, the name of the *Arabian Nights* princess who had battled a deranged sultan by dancing up a storm before his lascivious gaze.

Scheherezade's father, a trader in dry fruit, mainly raisins and figs, was either indifferent or callous. He was attached to his aristocratic wife in the city and their unpleasantly plump litter. Scheherezade's mother was useful during his business visits to the lime orchard. He'd stay for a couple of days, three maybe. Rukhsin warmed his bed and kitchen, and burnt in his arms. By contrast, the aristocratic wife was cold, lifeless. The lime orchard made him feel young, virile, in control. Next to the orchard, berries, tomatoes, lettuce grew in abundance, to be included in every meal with lamb meat. The trader ate as if there were no tomorrow, firing a round of burps after downing a jug of water.

Scheherezade was hostile to her father whose name she didn't care to repeat. Although he was the wealthiest trader in the province, he was miserly. With reluctance, he would provide for their clothes, schooling and meals. Scheherezade was convinced that her brother Bairam and she were as underprivileged as servants' children, which wasn't far from the truth. She saw her mother pressing her father's feet to lull him to sleep. Most nights, she would apply butter on his penis. Her mother moved to his demands, feigning ecstasy when he entered her...from the back, the front, both excited him; he was a dog in heat. Over time, the father looked at and fondled Scheherezade. Rukhsin snatched her away, a berry from the orchard which she wouldn't allow to be plucked. "Keep away from her," the mother hissed.

"She is not my daughter," he said bluntly. "You know that. She could be anyone's."

Rukhsin, practical to the core, avoided argument. Scheherezade pretended that she hadn't heard the man who might or might not have been her father. Her brother Bairam did not speak to the man either; he seemed to know more about their father than Scheherezade did. Bairam could list the trader's properties, the exact amounts he had stashed in which bank. Scheherezade didn't want to know more, although she did marvel whenever she saw the hulk insane with excitement before he clambered on top of her mother. Some day, some man would make love to her—but tenderly.That wish came true, or almost.

From her bed, the widow now gazed at the fading portrait...what a funny moustache. She had forbidden all her sons from sprouting moustaches. They had obeyed, no big deal for them. They hadn't taken sufficient care of her, they wouldn't even understand what the teacup meant to her, what her antecedents meant to her, what their father meant to her. The stupids. They hadn't ever asked her about where, why and when she had met their father. They didn't care. They didn't want to know of their parents' passage to India. "Their loss," she scowled, fidgeting on her grand bed.

∽

At 15, Scheherezade was married to an angel of a man, striking in his bearing and deportment. A poorly paid labour supervisor at a paper factory, he had a brow larger than a Yazd farmfield, his eyes chrome embers. That moustache, thick and bristly, excited her the moment she set eyes on her anointed groom. He would be her lover, her companion, her confidant. If he turned out to be brutal, so be it. She longed to be loved, embraced. She wanted to escape from the orchard. She had her mother's blessings, her brother's half curved smile...get out of here.

Expectedly her father, ever the trader detecting no profit, wasn't at the wedding *jashn*, enlivened by erotic folk songs exulting that the bride would be deflowered, she would bloom. She did.

Scheherezade and her angel Rustam Khushmandi lived in Teenar, an eight-hour walk away from Yazd. He worked by day at the factory, made love at night. Diligently. She expressed the right amount of pleasure, the right amount of naivete. She mastered the art of pleasing her man, and cooked with relish, an art she had already practised on her mother and brother. After meals, her groom nuzzled her neck; his moustache tickled her cheeks. She was sure this was the interlude of happiness ordained for her by the surer lines on her palms. Their love was ten-thousand-kisses deep. Within half a year of the wedding though, angel Rustam told her that he would rewrite their destiny. They would migrate. Where? Why? Can't be another home. She was worried; she lost that thrill of surrendering to his ceaseless kisses. Rustam told her about Hindustan. They had to go there as soon as they could. For a better upbringing for their child which had lodged itself in her Scheherezade's womb. Better? Could be worse.

Intuitively, Scheherezade felt wrong about quitting Iran. It was their home, their roots. Rustam retaliated crisply, "Women don't know what's good for them." She sulked for a few weeks, a few months month till she understood that he would leave anyway. She could not lose him; she could not disobey the father of her child. She addressed the most luminous star in the sky: she would leave with Rustam but she would always see the moon of Iran, wherever she was, hell or Hindustan.

Rustam had heaven on his mind for his Shezzy, as fragrant as freshly plucked flowers, as sweet as her concoction of tea coated with dairy cream. Whenever she desired to see him easy and groggy, she added a pinch of opium to the tea. Her brown eyes smiled, never mind if she was distressed. Her bosom swelled to his slightest touch. She was his poem, his reason to leave home with their unborn son.

Presumably, Hindustan was the promised paradise. Rustam's uncles, cousins, nephews, practically everyone from the Khushmandi clan, except its senile patriarch, had already left for Bombay. The immigrants prospered, they wrote letters home of the frothing ocean, of the thousands of rupees earned and spent. They extended Rustam generous invitations, not out of altruism entirely. Rustam was a tireless worker; he would be an asset to the clan's plans to establish their businesses far away from home. "Come Rustam, you shall receive. We're here, we are family," the letters of temptation chorused.

It was winter already, November 1928. All doubts repressed, Rustam and his Shezzy left by a steamer, *ishtimbar* they called it. The vessel's iron nose tilted loftily towards the clouds which had gathered on the steamer's departure. Passengers, amassed there thanks to discounted ticket rates, squatted in the pits of *SS Karamzad.* Scheherezade's account of the events to whoever cared to listen later was distinctly apocryphal. Nevertheless to her credit it never varied, her mouth opening and closing, the beak of a playful sparrow, when she recounted, "It rained hard as if the skies were angry, as if God didn't want us to go. The tide, the rain, lashed our faces like leather belts. I gave birth to my first child on that filthy *ishtimbar.* I was torn apart like a sheet of paper by women whose faces I can see to this day. They knew all the techniques of midwives. Finally I held my son, praying that he would drink of my breasts. I sang something which didn't make sense. I wept and then I laughed because my child's father looked so funny standing there. A big hairy walrus! Rustam would tell me that he carried me in his arms off the steamer, unconscious. We arrived in Dhobi Talao in a *tanga*, the horse was muddy brown. I clutched my baby, afraid that someone would snatch him away. When I opened my eyes, I saw peeling walls, a lizard on the ceiling as if nailed there. I looked out of the window; there was a balcony. I was told that the roads were empty as if a holiday had been declared to celebrate the birth of my son. The city wasn't crowded then. We were lodged in a house, as if by magic, with three rooms, a balcony, the house where I will breathe my last breath...if I can help it."

❧

Scheherezade gaped at the ceiling that Sunday morning. There was no lizard today, only yellow oil paint which had stopped peeling. Her sons slept. They always did for an extra hour on Sundays, God's special day for everyone except Scheherezade—a princess whom time had forgotten in a room, with her despicable cat and the cup that would have to be replaced but not with one of those hideous saucerless mugs. Not over her dead body. Tea was *not* made to be drunk from mugs. She folded the *chudder*, revelling in the craft of getting each fold crisper than her mood this morning. Her sons would wake up any minute. She would tell them of the cup. Her harangue would be gobbledygook. They would nod, look away, nod, look away. If only Rustam were here, he would have handled them, Rustam with that forest moustache which tickled her pale, vanishing cheeks. Her cheeks, once they were red apples. Rustam would sing to her in an Iranian dialect, "My little one, my little apple, my temptation, love me today, love me tomorrow, love me when you close your eyes. I'll kiss the velvet darkness of your gaze." Damn, those cataracts were jabbing again. She hated hospitals, injections, surgery more than she hated Gogoosh who had just murdered her cup of *chai*, her friend.

Friends...She hadn't known the intimacy of friends. *Never ever.* Striking friendships was as inconceivable as procuring a degree in education. Scheherezade had studied for a scant six years at Yazd's religious school run on charity by teachers ranging from the hopelessly surly to the exceedingly idealistic. Scheherezade had revealed a flair for languages, particularly English of which she had grasped a substantial vocabulary. She possessed an abridged English dictionary, a gift from her mother on her tenth birthday, a collection of stapled pages which she valued more than her few trinkets. She had memorised words but she would come unstuck at the letter 'a'. She would pass over to 'd', flip the pages some more, pleased that the letter 'q' hardly contained any entries. Quadrangle, quaff, queen, quick, quinine...that was easy. Her mother, Rukhsin had misgivings that her girl was a freak, her head cluttered with useless dictionary doodads. Rukhsin was as contemptuous of her children's friends—the few who were bold enough to step into the orchard house, a Y-shaped room with frayed rugs, decaying mattresses and a primitive cooking stove. On school holidays, Scheherezade would be joined infrequently by Pheroza, the postman's daughter. Naturally, Rukhsin disapproved. Pheroza was talkative and resentful at the slightest hint of reprimand.

"Do not invite her here," Rukhsin warned her daughter. "She is no good, she doesn't cover her head in front of me."

"She's my only friend," Scheherezade pleaded.

"You have your brother. I am there. You don't need friends," the mother ruled. "No friend has ever come to our help in distress and never will. Have I made myself clear. No friends please."

To be fair, Rukhsin wasn't an unyielding tyrant; she thought herself to be a protective mother. After all, she had located the angel groom for her girl; as a mother she had performed her duty. There was no point sending Scheherezade to school any more; she could sprout wings, fly away shamelessly. She could be misled by one of those gangly boys or by one of those raggedy teachers. Rukhsin understood that she didn't possess a shred of self-pride, she was a 'kept' woman. Scheherezade had also seen the postman with her mother. The way he had touched her suggested an erotic familiarity. The postman had caught Rukhsin's right hand, twisted it till she had winced with more pleasure than pain.

As much Scheherezade ignored her father, she ignored the postman as well. She longed to leave the house that smelt of limes and lettuce. Rustam was her ticket out. Frequently, he had noticed the girl crossing the marketplace. There was something melancholic, dignified about her. A proposal of marriage for Scheherezade was sent by Rustam's cranky father to Rukhsin who accepted the alliance instantaneously. Scheherezade was overjoyed...her *kismat* was about to change. She guessed that Rustam wanted her as much as she lusted for him, a man who would carry her away from her aloneness. She would take from the farm only three of her belongings: her prayer book of Ahura Mazda, the dictionary and her

Isfahan porcelain set of teacups and saucers, the only gift her father had ever given her in a fit of generosity on her 14th birthday. The trader had bragged about the bargain he had struck with the Isfahan street vendor. She would show off the tea set to Rustam Khushmandi. Scheherezade was sure that he would decode her every whisper attentively; she was certain that he would detect love in her eyes. After all she had given love to no one else, whatever love may or may not be.

Love, she could not summon up this Sunday morning for her four sons. Just see, just see those two louts—donkeys-monkeys—are sleeping. They didn't care if her teacup was dead, or if the woman who gave them birth was dead or alive. In fact, they would be relieved to see her off; she had hung on for too long. She wasn't ill, she didn't need doctors, the cataracts could be removed but the fog before her eyes didn't prevent her from seeing what they wanted most of all from her—a signature on a sheet of paper. They wanted to sell the *chai* shop, the Irani restaurant as such establishments are termed, grab the money, and leave her with Gogoosh.

Diamond Crown Restaurant and Stores was just a sneeze away on Dhobi Talao. She gaped at it every morning to check that it still existed. Her husband's treasure, her sons' burden. Along with two partners, Rustam Khushmandi had set up the shop circa 1940. Its specialty was a thick, minty sweet concoction, a Yazd recipe remixed. Tastes change. The shop was on lean days.

The sons had acquired a beer licence but the competitors were serving hard liquor in the same lane which kept thickening with chronic tipplers. Diamond Crown was an anachronism. It served mince cutlets and hot bread in the mornings to go as breakfast with the tea. The prices were affordable, the earnings at the end of each month disappointing. The Khushmandi Sons argued with their mother that, in additon, fast-food chains were on their way to steal their regular clients. There was no hope. Sons Jamshed and Mehernosh, who had not migrated, had turned grey sitting at the counters, each on eight-hour shifts. They wanted out. On her dead body. She would *not* let Diamond Crown go. Rustam's heart would have been broken, like her teacup

Rustam, dear Rustam. It didn't matter to their sons that their father left Iran to gift his children a future. Yazd had proliferated with Zoroastrians but the rest of Iran was presided over by the Shia-ite Muslims. If anyone in Yazd converted to Islam, Rustam had nothing but contempt for them. He would hang himself before changing his faith...or even think about it. It was prudent, Rustam would remind his princess, to quit Iran when they did. Triumphantly he would say that was the wisest decision he had taken in his life.

"Just see, just see, the bloody stupids aren't even aware of their parents' struggle for a better life," she sought sympathy from the ceiling. "These donkeys-monkeys take life as a given."

Hoisting herself out of the bed, she whimpered some more, "What use are sons? Perhaps a daughter would have taken me in her arms today. I wouldn't have felt isolated, helpless without my cup." She heard a shuffle. "Jamshed will make himself a tea-bag Darjeeling. Mehernosh doesn't even like tea...coffee he likes, black. They won't even ask me if I've had my *chai*."

There was a war in her heart that Sunday. She returned to the balcony and peered at the street below. No one had cleared the pieces of the teacup. That's alright. Perhaps tomorrow the pieces would be cleared by the municipal sweeper who wouldn't know its value. He would not have heard of Iran, the lime grove, mother Rukhsin, the trader father...*no one cares.*

Gogoosh, without her morning feed, gaped at Scheherezade with plaintive green eyes. She gaped back, softening "Wait, wait, wait, you'll get your milk, silly girl. I always do my duty. Don't think I'm broken like the cup. I'm a fighter."

Over a decade after the teacup tragedy, Scherezade Khushmandi died of old age in 2000.

The Irani *chai* shop survives. Jamshed and Mehernosh sit at the cash counter, eight hours each. They have preserved her copy of the Ahura Mazda, their moustachioed father's portrait...and her saucerless tea mug.

Two sons cared. That's why the moon of Iran still casts a light on Diamond Crown Restaurant and Stores.

A Prince in Time

Kabs was misunderstood. The prince-in-waiting fiddled while Samargarh burnt, circa 1978. He wasn't plugged into the state's woes—no time, no inclination, no ability—he had a headful of them to handle in Mumbai.

Rajkumar Kabir Pratap Singh was so misunderstood that his name would have been axed from the family tree if that were possible. He was to inherit the title of Maharaja of Samargarh through default. The reigning His Highness Dhairya Nath Singh, then 75-plus, had sired five daughters. His nephew, the closest male heir, was to inherit the title with an incalculable amount of property, jewellery, objets d'art, antiques and cash. Till the septuagenarian departed, the prince had to bide his time, acquire a soupçon of education and be worthy of a king's title in a nation where such titles are no longer constitutionally recognised.

Samargarh, a fairly prosperous province dotted with five hamlets, is served by a network of trains which halt in the state's capital, Samarner, daily but briefly. It is said to be an unshackled country but yesteryear's royalty command unflagging awe, genuflection and subservience. Every breath taken by the Samargarhis appears to be sanctioned by the *rajwadas*. When cavalcades of their cars—state flags fluttering—are driven at leisurely speed through the main town, the rest of the traffic freezes.

Timeless place, Samarner. *De jure* democracy co-exists with the *de facto* maharajas and maharanis, imposing palaces sometimes converted into dollar-trap hotels, diamonds the size of quail eggs, deep red velvet bedrooms, Tudor age drapes and secret *shikars* of the near-extinct chinkaras. The third post-Independence generation has either settled overseas, or returned home, some of them compassing their way to the Indian Parliament. Common. Very common. As common as the preternaturally servile inhabitants of Samarner where the septuagenarian maharaja's birthday is bugled in with a pineapple cream cake topped by a single blinking electric bulb, all documented fervently by TV crews, local and international.

For the people of Samargarh, escape from the extra-legal tutelage of their lords and masters was unthinkable. Let the royals be; let them be deified. Except for Rajkumar Kabir Pratap Singh aka Kabs, the future maharaja, who was rarely seen in his hometown. He hadn't built up a constituency of followers yet. Almost 22, he should have been straining at the leash to take charge.

Kabs drank, smoked grass, womanised, hosted rave parties aboard yachts, played roulette at Monte Carlo in summer and skied down Swiss slopes in winter. Wonderful. Still a college student, he was perfectly qualified to be the next maharaja—a good bad boy. Objections had repeatedly been raised to his prolonged absence from Samargarh. He ignored letters and phone calls from the state palace. Surely he could binge and orgy in the velvet chambers there. Retinues doggedly faithful to the state grumbled that besides fleeting visits, which could be counted on the fingertips, he remained anchored in Mumbai. He was tarnishing the name of the Samargarh clan, behaving as if the state didn't deserve him. Meanwhile, his debtors in Mumbai were multiplying faster than rabbits, his monthly bills shooting skywards. Kabs was a mess. He was misunderstood and liked it that way. "Only the mindless are uncomplicated," he cackled. "I'm a bunch of knots."

Mumbai could not contain him. His secretaries and domestic staff would resign after a year at most. Replacements were promptly brought in at double the salary. Hah, the city and its women captivated him.

Now a twist to the predictable plot. Royalty kids who go berserk while coming of age in Bombay—oh no, he wouldn't be one of those. Subconsciously perhaps—to give him the benefit of doubt—Kabs engineered a way out of completing his Bachelor of Arts degree from a Jesuit college. He challenged the Lit prof, who couldn't tell his James Joyce from Joyce Carol Oates, to discuss a chapter of *Ulysses* threadbare, lit up a joint during the preliminary exams, dared a priest to address the students on asexuality. "That Kabs is crazeee," moaned the teaching staff. He wasn't; he was just having a whale of a time. Satanically, he would spit out his first thoughts. Melodramatically he would strike a pose from the seat in the Junior BA classroom's last row. "Who am I? What am I? Why am I here?" he had sung operatically in the middle of a discourse on Sartre-Camus-Mann. "Who cares about these pseudos? I am out of here," he had left the room. Kabs was back on his seat the next afternoon but the priests had voted unanimously at a closed-door meeting to expel him with immediate effect. Before leaving the campus, he wandered off to the library, tore off his clothes behind a book rack, streaked through the library right down the corridor facing the principal's office and then stood still in the campus quadrangle, yelling, "Condemn me, O Holy Fathers! Hang me, kill me, destroy me!" And he wasn't even high on his noon gin-and-tonic.

A bunch of security guards rushed Kabs to his clothes. While buttoning his Levi's, he passed lewd remarks at the guards who were amused, shushing him as if he were an infant. No question of leaving the library. "I'll set myself on fire," he cautioned, flicking his Zippo lighter on and off. The priests were as shy of a scandal as they were of missing their daily prayers. Kabs had to be calmed, then either taken home or to a hospital. A doctor was summoned, the wild streaker pinned down by strong arms, injected with a tranquiliser and arm-carried to the sick room on the campus where he curled up and slept like a baby. The incident made it to the third page of the city's newspapers but the student's name was omitted at the request of the priests.

Going by the college records, it wasn't clear whether the father, mother or the septuagenarian maharaja had to be contacted in case of an emergency. None of them could be reached since phone lines in Samarner were down, expected to be repaired in a "few hours." So, in a kindly worded letter to his *guardians* in Samarner, it was recommended that Rajkumar Kabir Pratap Singh needed urgent clinical treatment.

Finally Rev Father DeLima managed to get in touch with Imroze Merchant who studied in another city college. The Reverend, often impressed by the unruly brilliance of his royal student, was aware that Imroze and Kabs—Tweedledee and Tweedledum—were inseparable in school. But but but...he didn't know that Tdee and Tdee hadn't been on speaking terms for two years if not more.

After being conjoined at the hips through ten years of school, Imroze had enrolled in a college, chosen unilaterally. It was Imroze's decision, no one else's. Incensed, Kabs had ranted right away, "Are you fucking mad? We can't go to different colleges. What'll I do without you? You're cut out for Humanities, the Arts, Culture, not bloody Economics in that ratty college. I'm for the Arts. I want you to be with me. Get it?"

Imroze couldn't follow a leader anymore. He had to become independent. No second thoughts about pursuing his family vocation: Chartered Accountancy it would have to be. If Kabs didn't like that, take a walk on the wild side, buddy.

Three evening vodkas down in his Italian-marbled apartment, Kabs snarled, "I pity you, Immy. All these years, you've been freeloading. I've bloody taken you to London and Geneva. What else do you want? Behave. Just keep guzzling my champagne, smoke my cigarettes, travel in my cars, wear the clothes I buy for you. Immy you know something? So many times money has been missing from my wallet. One thousand, two thousand, three thousand...you think I haven't noticed? You miserable, pitiable fellow...you're a thief...and now you want to go your own way. Go fucker, go."

When *fucker* left, Kabs dashed after him, "Sorry Immy sorry, I didn't mean that. Sorry. What the fuck do you want me to do? Beg?" Kabs would have begged if Immy hadn't rushed down the 12 flights of stairs. "Go, go, go but you'll never escape me."

Imroze had smarted. He could have killed Kabir with his bare hands right then but didn't because he understood the prince-in-waiting of Samargarh.

At New Delhi airport, three cars, secretaries Shamsher Bahadur and V Rathod, an unwieldy rose garland, a bouquet of chrysanthemums, an ice-box of champagne and a selection of wines awaited the Rajkumar and his reunited friend in case they were thirsty after the two-hour flight. It was a six-hour-long drive to Samarner. Arrangements for lunch had been made en route at Sunny da Dhaba famed for its *tandoor* cuisine. Reserved exclusively for an hour. High tea would await the Rajkumar and his friend on their arrival in the North Wing of Samargarh Palace. The more commodious South Wing was occupied by the ailing maharaja, his five daughters, four sons-in-law (one had died prematurely) and a cargo load of grandchildren. The East and West Wings had been leased to a hotel chain.

The secretaries outlined the itinerary before hitting the highway. Immy nodded. Kabs was too sedated to care. Immy slid into the front seat of the silver-grey Mercedes-Benz. Kabs sprawled on the backseat, chanting the eff word till he fell asleep like a baby again without a sound, and in rhythm with the bumps on the road.

They could have been mistaken for brothers: six feet, broad shoulders and foreheads, artists' hands, baritone voices and killer smiles in common. Immy didn't ease up while his friend slept. He understood that Kabs had to exorcise that independent, unruly part of himself to resurrect as the true prince. The high drama in college was contrived as a justification—more to himself than anyone else—for dropping out of college, and from the metropolis which had granted him the licence of free will.

He did not belong to a feudal state by choice but he did by birth. No escape. The Rajkumar could fiddle no more while his kingdom burnt. The enforced return of the prodigal was a self-scripted-directed act. That day the Rajkumar had worn jeans, a T-shirt and sandals. "Well played but Kabs you're fooling no one but yourself," Immy wanted to shake him up, but didn't and gazed instead at the blur of empty farmlands.

The Delhi-Samarner route was unexceptional like its cola advertisement hoardings planted at the edge of highways. Telephone numbers scrawled on walls promised quick cures for VD and erectile dysfunction. A Dr Palang Tod recommended his special blend of aphrodisiac guaranteed to make geriatrics break bridal beds. Trucks were overtaken perilously by the driver who mumbled cuss words under his breath, apologising when Imroze flashed him a censorious look. Aah there it was, Sunny da Dhaba. The entourage was respectful of royalty but they too had to eat, drink and take a leak. Secretary Shamsher Bahadur downed beer since Kabs was asleep. Imroze smoked a cigarette and refused food irritably when secretary Rathod bansheed, "But Sir, you must have something. You must be hungry."

"I am not. Thank you," Imroze said with finality.

The secretaries could sense that Imroze was eager to deliver his friend home, so they brusquely rounded up the entourage which had to complete three more hours of the road trip. Imroze was about to crush his dying cigarette when Kabs snatched it and inhaled deeply, "Hey, the *dhaba*...man...and thou beside me. Just like old times Immy. Now come, come, come, hug me tight. What're you waiting for? Hug me!" Kabs stamped out the cigarette with the heel of his shoe, flung his arms wide open and hugged Imroze. He held on to Imroze, weeping uncontrollably, "Forgive me, my friend. Forgive me for the shit I said. Please forgive me. I couldn't bear the thought of you abandoning me for another college. I can be such a twit. I've missed you so much...so much."

"Kabs, it's alright."

"No it isn't...and tell me, tell me, tell me, have you missed me all these days?"

Imroze hugged Kabs tighter, "Of course I missed you."

"How much? How much did you miss me?"

"A lot Kabs...missed you every day."

"I missed you every hour, every minute..."

The two held on to each other till Imroze realised that the secretaries were gaping at their extended embrace.

For the rest of the ride, the school friends talked like children—in incomplete, excited sentences about the days that were. "I can never forget how you quietly went and locked up Mr Hazarnis in the loo," Kabs tittered. "You were so damn good at painting, you were his pet Immy...and you went and did that Judas number on him."

"Hello! But you did that to Hazarnis...not me," Imroze was about to correct the Rajkumar but didn't.

*

Imroze Merchant was visiting Samargarh Palace for the second time. Little had changed. The three-storey salmon stone façade had a Spanish castle motif: *khakhi* walls, a terraced roof with stubby spires, round turret with carved *jharoka* windows at the centre and corners—a U-shaped structure with an enormous three-pronged courtyard dominated by shade granting trees, bushes, shrubs, flower beds, six whooshing water fountains and a gazebo at the far-end of the courtyard. The gate was of solid glossy black iron, bearing the royal insignia of lions in red-white-and-blue. The hotel's guests, mostly European, ambled about in *kurta*s, loose *churidar*s, wind-cheaters and straw hats. Some men wore Bermudas despite the winter chill. It was just another evening at the hotel-cum-royal-residency except, of course, for the arrival of the black sheep, about to be sprayed spotless white.

Imroze had been polite throughout the ride. Politeness can be interpreted as approval. Before they alighted from the car, he had to articulate his opinion, "Kabs you've been resisting this palace for years. If you ask me, you've tricked everyone—the college priests, me, even yourself. I can see through your game...you want to be royalty, a raja-maharaja. For years you've said you wouldn't give up your independence but you're no different from them. You could do so many things in the outside world. That palace... it's your death wish. You'll never be the same again."

Kabs grimaced, "Let it pass Immy. You know I'm a bunch of knots. I have to untie myself. I have no great regard for democracy that I should worry about palaces, feudalism and all that crap. This is the way it is, pal. We are the rajas-maharajas you read about in history books. You're judgemental and I like that. Someone cares. You're right; you're just about to lose your friend. If possible remember me well." Kabs had surrendered to centuries-old customs and conventions. Someday soon, he would be a raja.

Had he wanted, Kabs could have been educated at universities abroad like his forebears; he could have bought prime education and friendship of a dozen Imrozes anywhere. Instead, the Samargah state committee comprising uncles, cousins and assorted advisors had sanctioned Mumbai where an eye could be kept on the boy who was far too impetuous for their comfort. At high school he broke every rule in the book but topped the examinations every year. Didn't cram for exams, no way. He was born brainy, analytical, observant. He devoured books, could expostulate for hours on art—Rembrandt, Da Vinci, Pollock were his gods. He could *think* and that was dangerous for the Samargarh clan. His parents had been advised time and again to coerce him to return to the palace, pay obeisance to the maharaja on his wheelchair and become a familiar face in the state populated largely by wheat farmers, metal traders and the nouveau riche class of property owners. Royalty's dominance over the landed *zamindars*, the new generation yuppies and the cash-rich farmers had to be preserved if not consolidated: feasible only with a dynamic maharaja in the half-preserved palace. Kabs was the best of a bad lot of potential successors. He had to be tamed, fall in line. He had to monitor the balance sheet of the annual revenues earned by Samargarh from its assets, investments and the share in hotel profits, all of which were dwindling.

Alcohol, drugs and sexual aberrations went with the territory, the palace committee reiterated, but this Rajkumar was incorrigible. He had ignored the palace cabal's letters and phone calls for so long that it was insulting to the committee. Once news spread of the streak scandal, the committee was upbeat, "See this was bound to happen. Rajkumar Kabir Pratap Singhji went mad at that college. He belongs here. A graduation degree would have gone well after his name but we can get him that with a correspondence course. Simple!"

The committee led by his paternal uncle, Manendra Singh welcomed the Rajkumar at the entrance to the North Wing. *Tilak* and *haldi* were applied to his forehead. Cousins, turned out in *sindoor,* red saris, touched his feet chorusing, *"Khamaghani, khamaghani"*; elderly women wept with some form of inflicted happiness. The Rajkumar was marched right into the maharaja's chamber where he kneeled before the old man in a wheelchair. Maharaja Dhairya Nath Singh touched the Rajkumar's head, and announced telegrahically, "Your wedding. Next month. Daughter. Bandor *gharana*. Bless. Bless."

The Rajkumar acquiesced without a word of protest, *"Jee Maharaj."* That assent received, the Rajkumar's parents Pratap Dhairya Nath Singh and Ragini Pratap Dhairya Nath Singh, entered the chamber which smelt of medicines and the nurse's cologne, to seal the marriage. A photograph of the Bandor girl, framed in a silver valentine, had been kept for the Rajkumar in his chamber. Dispassionately Imroze watched the flow of events, which must have taken under 10 minutes. This is the way it is in *raj gharana*s, at least in Samargarh. A life on control was predestined for his friend, and his parents kept at a distance. The Rajkumar rarely spoke about them; they were handmaidens at the announcement of their son's wedding.

Manendra Singh, the regent-like uncle, was cold and distant with Imroze Merchant, who was escorted by the palace attendants to his room for the night. Early morning, he would be driven to New Delhi airport to catch the late afternoon flight back to Mumbai. His friend did not ask him to stay on for another day, offering a handshake instead, "Thanks Immy for everything. I'll see you in the morning...for sure...before you leave." Dinner would be sent to Imroze's suite on a trolley. Manendra Singh led the guest away from the Rajkumar, saying magnanimously, "Do help yourself to the mini-bar in the fridge. Good night."

A friend of 10 years discarded like a paid escort. Imroze watched television in his room, barely registering the visuals or sounds. He mixed himself three Scotch-and-sodas from the mini-bar, crept into bed around midnight and was ready to leave at 6 a.m. after a toast-and-tea breakfast. A taxi was waiting but Kabs was nowhere in sight. Affronted, Imroze asked the attendant, "Isn't he awake? I have to see him before I go." No way. *Rajkumar hukum* was asleep. There were express orders not to wake him up.

The taxi slowly rolled out of the gate. From an old rickety Ambassador, Imroze turned back for a parting look at the palace. He thought he saw Kabs on the terrace, waving him farewell. Imroze wasn't sure and didn't wave back. It made more sense to disconnect from the time-warp which covered Samargarh Palace.

As soon as the taxi moved out of the gate, the driver said sombrely that *Rajkumar hukum*'s father had requested a meeting—wouldn't take more than 15 minutes of his time. It was on the way—at Neelgarh Haveli. *Haveli* was a misnomer; the taxi drove into a squat, limestone structure, a modest farmhouse at best. The slim white columns holding up the house were deeply veined. The dark, sunless interiors required an immediate coat of white paint. Yet there was no mistaking the royal signs, especially the ornate silver-framed photographs of Kabs as a child and as a young man; the parents with the son showing off a tennis racquet. Kabs may have been sporty in that photograph but otherwise described sport as mere grist for the television channels. Paintings of ancestors in royal regalia hung tiredly on the wall; the state's crest was faintly visible on the crockery used to serve Imroze coffee and biscuits. It was a bright wintry sun outside but the drawing room's lights had to be switched on so that the father could see his son's friend.

Pratap Dhairya Nath Singhji was handsome, taller and with features sharper than his son, goateed, with a thick crown of white hair and diamond-studded ears. His face was unlined, tanned and pleasant. His teeth flashed a blinding smile at his son's friend who performed a jejune version of the traditional *khamaghani.* Pratapsinghji dismissed the attendants and began with a round of politesse: the weather, the newspaper headlines that morning and ceaseless inflation. Graceful old man but Imroze had to reach New Delhi well in time for the flight and checked his wrist watch pointedly.

"Sorry Imroze," Pratapsinghji shifted gears to the topic of the morning. "I will come straight to the point. My wife and I will always be under your obligation. You have been our Rajkumar's only friend for so many years. Often you have been a sobering influence. We did not meet him, often in accordance with the protocol decreed here but we were constantly updated about what our son was up to."

Imroze said sincerely, "You don't have to thank me. Kabir has been a wonderful friend. Please look after him, Sir."

"It must have been eight or ten years ago when you were at the palace."

"Ten, Sir."

"You haven't changed at all but Kabir is a different person. Without you, perhaps he would have derailed. I would say right till the end of school, you were his conscience-keeper."

"You give me too much credit, Sir. Kabir is capable of achieving so much. If I may say so, it's a pity that he has to return here to become a raja...how long will this farce of a kingdom last? He is capable of anything...he can chuck it all up...and..."

"No chance of that. He will adapt. All of us have to conform."

"Sir, Kabir can break rules. He cannot make them."

"Even I thought that way, Imroze," Pratapsinghji continued in his benign tone. "But everything, right down from my education and my marriage to the future of my only son, has to be in accordance with the rules of the state. Or else we will stop existing."

"You still believe yourself to be royalty?"

"You could say that."

"Sir, the British left but royalty still has these illusions that there can be no end to dynasty rules."

"A dynasty can rule a democracy too, Imroze."

"Sir, today it's a new world out there...we aren't ruled by kings...and if we are, we ought not to be. Royalty could stop existing," Imroze hectored.

"Not in our lifetime. Anyway shall we wind up, son? You have a long ride ahead. I wanted to express our gratitude...our thanks."

"I don't accept your gratitude or your thanks, Sir. How can you just hand your son away? He will not be happy at all...he will suffocate."

The father didn't flinch. "I did not give my son away. He was taken over. Would I rather see him as the head of this state or as a moody boy wasting his life away? He has to get what is rightfully his. He must perform his duties to the state...and to his parents. Let me see you to the taxi. I will not thank you again but I will say one thing...you are the only one who understood Kabir."

Pratapsinghji's wife emerged from a shadowy room, an attractive woman in floral chiffon and tinted-brown hair cut to the shoulders. She offered Imroze a box of sweets, *prasad* from the morning *puja,* with the entreaty that he should share it with his parents. Outside the *haveli,* Pratapsinghji handed him a velvet box holding six gold coins stamped with the royal crest of Samargarh.

"These can only be kept within the family," he said sincerely. "You've been like a brother to our Kabir. Please do keep them. If you say no, we will be very hurt."

As the taxi left the *haveli,* Pratapsinghji waved at Imroze like Kabs may or may not have when Imroze was leaving the palace.

The ostentatious invite which landed up at Imroze's home a month later for Rajkumar Kabir Pratap Singh's wedding was personally signed by Maharaja Pratap Dhairya Nath Singh. Imroze neither attended the event nor the Rajkumar's subsequent coronation.

Once in a while, though, he would gaze at the six coins—the price of losing a friend.

Father, Lost and Found

Suddenly Rehaan was the age of his imagined father. 40. The story was, is, that he had never seen his father, never felt his breath on him. He did not know whether his father was kind, cruel, tall, short, wonderful, terrrible, ugly. An android. A pod. Hatehimhimhim. His father was a ghost as ubiquitous as Banquo. Some said he was alive in another part of town, bastard, or maybe domiciled in another town, country, with another family. Damndamndamn he could be anyone, anywhere, nowhere.

I, his semen...sex, bed, wham wham, wrinkled baby howls, was born at St Elizabeth's Nursing Home. Nice. Indeed the safest place to be born, supervised by nuns of Mona Lisa smiles but father wasn't a palpable memory. He was there, faceless, formless, brainless, shapeless, a presence playing truant.

Adult, still a child, Rehaan was employed as a reporter with a no-brow Bombay eveninger vended whimsically at 10 in the morning. Baby-faced Rehaan cursed and blessed. No one answered his questions unless he was interviewing them formally for the silly all-colour Sunday section—What do you eat for breakfast? What do you dream of? What are your bloodybloodybloody hobbies? Say cheese you burger, pick pad and pen, scram from those chocolate box apartments, colonial bungalows...Jacuzzi penthouses ..Swiss-architecture chalets...Venetian villas...What to call them?...What to call celebs? Tacktacktacky.

Yoked to journalese—his first vocation—Rehaan jerked robotically through the 500-word deadlines, eyes wide open, mind tight shut. Loved and hated the rue, rue, routine. Silly people with silly mind twists, he'd cackle when no one could hear, admitting auto-critically that he was the silliest. A loser.

Till he could find and hug....hug?...his phantom father, callous, mean, indifferent father, Rehaan Raahil Jaffar was a son on a pedestrian beat.

Rehaan was either mentally backward or fabulously intelligent. He could have been an intellectual, an academic; he had this gift for deconstruction-reconstruction, was sufficiently well read—Sartre, Camus, Borges, Chomsky—over-average at the very least. A fanatic for Steinbeck's grapes, a post-graduate in Sociology, aware of the difference between Foucault and Bourdieu he could snap out an edit on the Left, Right or the Pink commissioned by lofty journals which couldn't pay him for a single word. On occasion, he would be remunerated with token book coupons, allowing him to own discounted editions of Gorky, Gogol and Premchand translations. He did and didn't need these but he needed his father, to know him if not possess him.

He hadn't been told much about his father. Or his mother for that matter. Rehaan's bio-plot could never thicken. Grandfather, a retired bank manager, given to playing the martyr to the hilt, anguish streaming through a grid of wrinkles, would narrate news report-style, "Your mother died while giving birth to you. Poor thing did not even see your face. Bad luck. She married without my consent, she died without my consent. I took charge of you."

Grandfather omitted to add, "That's all from the newsroom tonight." The retired man's cupboard had skeletons which he would not exhume. His teenaged daughter had eloped with one of his bank's junior trainees. Never trust these upstarts. See what the *namak haraam* did. That skunk should have died of his curses, not his daughter who must have been either deluded or drugged by that rotter. Should have been arrested.

Rehaan didn't contradict his grandfather, so lovable with his jug-handle ears, his thick, centre-parted hair, his gap-toothed smile which he described as 'Gateway of India', and most of all, his habit of breaking into vintage, tremulous film songs whenever he'd gulped an Old Monk too many.

Snatches of grandfather's songs always underscored his disappointment with life. Nothing changes, the damn humdrum beat goes on. The moon, the stars and the seasons wouldn't mourn his loss when he ups and leaves for the heavens. For some unilateral reason, grandfather discouraged any mention of the Bandra suburbs. *NO BANDRA PLEASE?* Nutty grandfather, adorably nutty. Just another quirk like he would not permit alphonsos in the house, a reasonably comfortable three-roomer on Sleater Road, next to the railway station, west.

Mangoes, he believed, bred worms in the stomach. They were forbidden fruit. No, no, his response to the very mention of Bandra was no quirk, Rehaan suspected. Father—that bank trainee must be a pasha after all these years, living it up on Pali Hill, Carter Road, Bandstand, as handsome as a fairytale prince. Come on grandfather, Rehaan would beg for the address a clue, a lead. Tellmetellmetellme.

"If you love me, don't ever ask me about the past," he'd repeat at times, as if he were reciting the penultimate line of a poem. Then reclining into a red *maqhmal*-uphostered chair, he would sniffle into a hand towel, its edges already wet with his tears. "Men don't cry," he would proclaim. "But I do and I am proud of it. Just goes to show that I am human. Not hard-hearted like your *asli* father."

This was difficult. If Rehaan were to ask about his father, he would be guilty of ingratitude to the man who had raised him as a son. If he suppressed his curiosity, that would be unnatural. Perhaps that's why he looked for surrogate fathers. When a senior editor shared his lunch box of neatly folded *rotis*, gifted him a book or a shirt, Rehaan imagined...father must be like him. Yet, the son kept a distance, conscious that such a surrogate relationship would be emotionally transient. Yesyesyes, he needed to talk to someone about his search still not undertaken, he needed an Agony Daddy.

Enough, get on with yet another interview, yet another duller than a dull press briefing at the Public Works Department's head office. On which planet are you *abba*? *Abba* stop this game, you hide, I seek for how long?

Would Rehaan call his father *abba?* Probably not though it sounded apt. He wanted to respect someone, anyone as long as the candidate fitted the slot. Mixed-up, cross-wired, Rehaan slapped himself verbally. He forgot about Sociology; wasn't asked to hack out edits anymore—his superiors reserved the gravitas for themselves. Rehaan, Rehaan, he tends to get into prosaic platitudes. So he was back to quizzing men and women half his age, about their hang-ups and hobbies. Rehaan was 40, 40, 40. Still no news, no abracadabra *abba* from Bandra.

Then grandfather died. After a walk in the rain on the Marine Drive seafront—where he would once take his daughter for strolls—he burnt with fever for days and closed his eyes stubbornly as if he didn't want to see the sunlight anymore. Now he could have given *abba*'s address to Rehaan. He tried, "Can you tell me his name... where he is?" This time he didn't reprimand the grandson but smiled through that Gateway of India magisterially—ask him anything but that.

And he was gone.

Grandfather, grandfather, tell me, please tell me. At his graveyard Rehaan cried into a hand towel. The grandson, no son, felt better for crying, always did. It made him feel his heart was still ticking.

No sensational career leaps, no earth-changing edits, only interviews. Rehaan, just handle the local beat, will you? In charge of city reporting, Rehaan was into the north, east, west, south suburbs. He shifted from Sleater Road. No more fast Borivli-Churchgate trains soft rocking the foundations of Hamdard Building, *no one* wondering if he'll be home for dinner...should it be kept in the fridge?

Rehaan lived alone in Bandra East, Patrakar Nagar, where every journalist knew exactly what he ate, drank and his relationships with women he longed to love but not hold for a lifetime. Neither did any one of them offer to darn his socks, slice the huge amounts of mangoes he now stored rebelliously in straw baskets during the summer months. The women—let's see there were three of them at various stages of his post-grandfather phase—did not tolerate his fits of anger directed mostly at himself for not being valued to the degree he deserved. Who does he think he is? Godgodgod.

Women, men...he fleetingly experimented with bisexuality. And *abba*...who needs *abba?* Too late Rehaan understood that he did need relationships. Single and lonely, he began to drink much more than his moderate two vodka tonics on Sunday evenings. He needed to know.

Damn you *abba*, damn. He had his father's name but was convinced that the name had been coined by the martyr grandfather. He could have placed an entirely cryptic ad in the newspaper, beseeching his father to own up to him. He could write a read-between-the-lines-article on a turd of a father. Can't, his newspaper colleagues would sneer. They're brainless but not *thaaaat* brainless. Rehaan was not greying but the two parallel creases on his forehead had deepened into turrets...that soul-crushing newspaper job...and *abba abba abba*. Stressedout man, stressedout.

Contacts in the police echelons didn't help. Anyway he didn't want to tell them his story. So he obfuscated his search for an unknown *abba* by recording his FIR statement as a third-person account. There is a certain friend who wants to know where his father could be, could they help? That sort of a thing. Blank cop faces. He tried the route of e-mail blogs, veiling his identity. No progress. Only some invitations of sex for money—blow job, erotic massage or did he need the whole treatment? Full night, negotiable charge.

Rehaan had slipped into the Bandra East world effortlessly. A chameleon not sure about his *wajood, karma, kismat*. "All the same, you asshole," masochistically he'd insult his reflection in the mirror. No moustache, clean face, smile a dentist's delight. Grow up boy, grow up, those forehead creases aren't helping.

He had severed connections with all his aunts, uncles, grand-aunts and more of the ilk. They hadn't been civil to his grandfather, the creeps. He disliked them vehemently; they hadn't been welcome to the Sleater Road home. They would send over *kheer* and *batasha*s on Eid, but these festive tokens would be handed over to the neighbours or fed to stray cats. Grandfather forbade Rehaan from fraternising with his uncles-aunts-nephews-nieces. He would fume, "When I'm dead and gone, don't let those *daayan*s and *shaitan*s get to you. Swear on my head on this."

Once he was dead and gone, Rehaan waited, no hurry. If he'd waited for so long, a few months didn't count. Yet he knew that he would have to speak to at least one of the family *shaitan*s to understand why they had attended grandfather's funeral, patted him on the back and left as soon as their duty was over—as if they were professional mourners. They hadn't lingered.

"Because, he would have liked it that way," grandfather's nephew, Jabbar, insisted. "There was a time when he would visit us on Eid, then he stopped without any explanation. Still, he was a *neq* man, he gave up everything for you. Did you know he didn't ever remarry because of you?"

"That he would never let me forget."

"He didn't want any woman to ever take you away from him," Jabbar narrated. "He was afraid because..."

Jabbar and Rehaan hadn't touched their double espressos in one of those look-alike coffee shops dotting Bandra Bandstand.

Jabbar looked away, "You're a grown-up man. You've made something of your life. You're well connected. By now you must know something at least."

"I don't, please tell me whatever you know."

"Not much."

"Anything, something."

"Your father's name...Bhushan Bhalla."

"What?"

"A Hindu from Meerut...you know that."

"All this religion stuff doesn't matter to me. Is he still alive?"

"Yes."

"Did he marry again, does he have children?"

"He has three children, all doing well. One daughter married, two sons abroad. Bhalla's wife is there also, pleasant lady I'm told."

"Have you ever met her...him?"

"No."

"Then how do you know?"

"He got in touch with me some 10-12 years ago; he wanted to meet you. I told him it would be better to leave you alone...with your grandfather..."

"Why?"

"Your grandfather would have wanted it that way. He was afraid, very afraid that you would..."

"What?"

"Old people...*buzurghs*...are afraid of being left alone"

"I would have never left him alone."

"Yes but who is to tell a *buzurgh* that? He loved you."

"But..."

"He was very god-fearing, remember that. His daughter got involved with someone outside our faith. He could forgive her anything but that...a boy...a *kafir*. He wouldn't have let you follow any other faith.

"I don't believe this.That's hardly the issue."

Getting up, Jabbar said quietly, "Isn't it the issue? *Allah haafiz*," and left a note with an address.

It was 3 p.m., just an hour left for Rehaan to clock in at the newspaper office. The hour was right for him, auspicious even, to just walk over to his father's address at Pali Hill, go straight up and then second turn to the right. Jabbar had chosen the venue for their meeting thoughtfully.

Abba would be surprised, he'd be glad for sure, he'd call for tea, a slice of cake. He'd pull Rehaan to his heart. They wouldn't require words or religion.

Rehaan's life would be redefined.

Without any drama, he scanned the seafront, the waves continuing their afternoon pirouettes. Why is the sea so potent for reappraisal, for liberation from doubts. Why, why, why?

Rehaan was sure that he was the only 40-plus child in the world. Doesn't matter. He'd have someone to respect, someone to talk to, someone to quarrel with on trivialities, someone who'd say, *"Beta."* He wanted to hear that so much. Someone to tell him to quit drinking.

He left the café, forgetting to settle the bill. "Newspaper guy," the head waiter grumbled, "*saalas*, they don't pay."

He walked through the zigzag lanes, leaving his car parked on the seafront. Pay and park. Fragmented thoughts played out in his head: "*Grandfather my dear grandfather* you should have told me. I would have understood, I would have loved you more deeply than I did. I would have, I would have...It's not your fault, it's my mother's fault. She didn't listen to you, didn't think of me. She defied you...how could she? Independence is one thing, responsibility another. Wherewherewhere would I have been if you hadn't taken charge?"

"*Abba* must be seventyish," Rehaan conjectured. He would look after Bhushan Bhalla from this afternoon. His sons must hardly be around; these NRI types never are. On their holidays his grandkids must be chewing *abba*'s head up. How thrilled he would be to see his first-born, his lost-and-found son. Thrilled if that's the right word, maybe something more.

The wiry security guard at the apartment building asked whom he wanted to see. Rehaan said, "Bhalla *saab*," the name sounding as if it were his legacy.

"What work do you have with him?"

Rehaan fished out his visiting card, saying strongly, "Journalist *hoon main*, appointment *hai*."

The security man, not the sort to spoil an afternoon with an altercation, drawled, "*Jaao*."

The elevator took its time. The marbled foyer was empty. Rehaan wished he'd had a whisky...too late too late. He had to look emotionally stable. He couldn't get wound up, not today, a day of reunion. Oh *abba,* we will laugh, we will be happy, I'll be happy, he'll be happy, we'll be happy.

The automatic elevator deposited Rehaan to the fifth floor. Automatic, big deal. There was a hush, no indication of what kind of a welcome awaited him.

Rehaan didn't ring the doorbell. He looked out of the corridor's window. The sea tide was low, comforting. It would be there, unchanged, the way his grandfather sang one of those morose vintage songs. The tides wouldn't change after he was gone.

Grandfather, see your Rehaan now, about to become a man today. Some things can change. If grandfather were alive, he would have been upset, betrayed. He had guarded the boy for years, decades. Rehaan had been his wealth, his possession, his act of faith, his religion.

Rehaan was outside the door. *Go ahead, ring the damn doorbell.*

He didn't move.

Unbroken stillness behind the door. The elevator carried a family to another floor. They looked at Rehaan, looked away, formulating a decision. Perhaps he's a visitor, never seen him before.

Rehaan didn't have any promises to keep. Grandfather was no longer around; nothing and no one could diminish his love for the old man. At this moment Rehaan was about to be released...from him, from his own prison...of questions.

There was no voice to prompt him to go ahead.

From the window, the Bandra seafront was watchful.

Pause.

Rehaan about-turned, walked very normally—neither brisk nor slow—down the five flights of stairs. Alone again, a moment of self-pity, then surprising relief, as if a long-postponed surgery was over.

The security guard asked, *"Saab mila kya?"*

Rehaan nodded, "Yes."

He returned to the city beat, drove to the office an hour away as if he were driving through air: the newsroom hummed with breaking stories of murders, robberies, showdowns in the state assembly, a suicide, extortions, man-made and natural calamities. Yet Rehaan smiled. He smiled at his reporting team, "So any sensational stories today?"

"No, boss," a reporter yawned. "It's just another day."

To Dream or Not to Dream

Crimson oceans open up; yellow submarines are grounded; the dead are reborn; the living are dead; the skies rain rose petals. Rows of skyscrapers shrink to the height of dwarfs; flame-and-arrow battles are fought on the streets; winds dance. The Taj Mahal is painted electric blue; the Gateway of India goes brinjal purple. Hands turn into tentacles, feet fins, eyes hard boiled eggs.

Intermission.

Popcorn. Cola fizz. Multiplexes in Borivli screen Bangkok porn. A thousand hands strangle an unidentified neck; a faceless man asphyxiates in a car-park basement. A masked woman performs a split-second jazz ballet in 3-D. Pugs converse on cell phones. Blackberries ping. Forest trees from Macbeth *march through a snowscape. Street kids sell computer-age magazines. A sip of cocoa is laced with arsenic; a funeral cortège winds down Delhi's India Gate; a ghost rises from the crypt...*

Wake up, wake up, it's another dream. It's over. Daniel could drink a glass of water, go back to sleep, start another dream. For nights without any let-up, he experienced a new disaster movie every night, each worse—or better—than the preceding one. He couldn't remember the details or he would have taken notes.

At the year-end, 2011, a month full of dreams was stoking his subconscious. He remembered them in vignettes, never the beginning or the middle. The endings stayed for a while—till his first cup of coffee. His dream notes would have been entertaining. Not to anyone but himself. These weren't nightmares; these were dreams. He had dreamt of wars, torture chambers and riots before but never regularly. This was getting ridiculous. One of the dreams was in black-and-white with him prancing in Van Gogh's field of sunflowers drained of colour.

The widescreen in his mind was active, running a late-night show regularly. After endless nights of these dream flicks, he tried to switch off the projector. No more random images, please. No more unspooling of disconnected scenes shabbily scripted and edited at tortoise pace. Now hadn't he also seen a tortoise morphing into a panther? And that werewolf cricketer playing solo at the stadium, bowling and batting alone? A game of patience? Horribly hazy, the innings had ended with a fleet of Rolls Royces smashing into a wall of no return. Crash 22, a neon-sign had said. Putrid pun.

Yoga *asanas*, a gel shave and a shower were followed by an address to his reflection in the mirror. Danny was a playwright and stage director. Soliloquies to him were as natural as breathing.

Dear dear Danny, you're not alone. You've got yourself for company. You're not losing your marbles. Don't get paranoid now. You're having the time of your life: it's a bowl of cherries, apricots, carrots. You're gambolling through the glades; you're quite saturnine, you know. Could kiss you right now...mwaaaahaaamwaah.

You look smarter than you ever did in your youth. You're dishy; silver-streaked hair which that gorgeous Mulatto hair designer in Cape Town had refused to colour. "You have a long neck Sir. This hair is you, god given, perfect. Dye it and it'll be ruined," she had raved in a voice outraged at the very thought of tampering with his two-month-old crop. "Maybe I'll trim the sideburns a teeny bit," she had capitulated.

You loved it, you loved it, you chump, you narcissist. That's why you gave her a tip which could have bought her for the night. Now now Danny boy...one-track mind.

You don't need dreams. You're respected—arguable, arguable. You don't drink to forget like you did; you've quit smoking; sex is regular (extremely arguable). It all depends on your travels. Right? Simpler to get laid outside the city. Amsterdam...Danny that's where you should have been born. Smoke joints by the canals, pick your entertainment for the night, ordered by room service. Hey you horny bastard, what's wrong with you? Zip up.

You have a loyal set of three friends. Make that two, at last count. You don't need anyone. Apply the brakes this very minute. Whom are you kidding? Come on, admit it. You want someone to need you, want you, lust for you, love you. That's it.

That bloody love shit could be the reason for your December of dreams.

Daniel R Monteiro was a Roman Catholic. His father, a stalwart theatre stage designer, had died of alcoholism. His mother Albetty, a chorus dancer in the movies, raised her Danny still in his knee-pants as a devout Christian, saw him through an unaffordable convent school education and an economics graduation degree from Leeds University, Britain. Not quite Oxford but count your blessings: Leeds offered a scholarship. Oxford didn't.

Albetty slept around with senior clerks, actors' secretaries and assistant directors at studios till she was 50. For years, she owned the key to a make-up room on the first storey of Shabistan Studio. She didn't hide her sidebar and more lucrative profession from her son. He didn't feel ashamed of his mother at all. She had no choice; she did what she did for him. No two or three ways about it: she would simply not have been admitted to the chorus line, or the studio, had she objected to an assistant director's caveat. "You will have to make compromises," he had said mechanically, surveying her from toe to top.

"No one's forcing you. If interested, come tomorrow. Or else, ta ta bye bye baby."

Originally from Mangalore, Albetty, the background micro-item of a thousand dances, was now senile, confined to an old people's home in Bengalaru. It was expensive but Daniel would have bought the Buckingham Palace for his mother if she had ever asked him to. He cherished the scene she enacted on his birthday each year before marching off to church: she would cry into her lace handkerchief, and await her son's reaction, "Your dad was a fine man. God calls those whom he loves early." The son would look appropriately glum but not cry. Mum Albetty would never fail to congratulate him for his dry eyes, trilling, "Wonderful. It's a gift. Don't ever cry. The day I go, smile when you place a wreath at my grave. I do want that wreath, don't forget Danny."

Dear Danny, you won't dream tonight, not to worry. Your mother's courage is with you; her supplications to the Almighty have been for you. Exclusive. Say a little prayer before you sleep tonight. Sleep early. You must call up Aunty Thelma. She'll tell you which prayer exactly. Now get going, you're already late for the rehearsals.

This play's a bitch. That man who calls himself a producer is a vampire...those bloodied fangs of his! Imagine, he has the nerve to tell me, "Mr Monteiro, you will not use real flowers in the finale. Fresh flowers are too expensive. Paper flowers, paper flowers chalega.*"*

Mad, mad, MAD. Penny wise pound foolish. Keeps provoking you...insane. Take away the crystal decanter you've loaned the production; your embroidered kurta*; sweatshirt from Marks & Spencer; the Swarovski vase. You must have been fruits and nuts to give them to the cretin. Show that chap what a MOWRAWN he is.*

Go now GO or the roads will get choked.

Now do you really have to drive that far? It's been a year, he's making the entire cast...you...hang on for who knows what. Imagine, he has even declared...tan tan na... to the press that he will stage Billis, *the Indian adaptation of* Cats, *next year. Needs a reality check. Keeps saying,* "Sab ka band bajaa dega?" *Take a walk, you dolt.*

Anyway who cares what he does or doesn't. Why can't his production guys or whatever they are, have the rehearsals closer to your house? Danny boy, you're the director, dammit.

The director's family, Mrs Francis D Monteiro, and their children David, Frank and Marlene, were in Ontario, Canada. He had dual citizenship; his chartered accountant had recommended an NRI status for tax reliefs. The birth of the three kids had been strategised: Frances travelled three months ahead of *the day* to Ontario every time her stomach swelled and rumbled. David, Frank and Marlene were natural-born Canadians.

Years ago, Mrs Monteiro taught history in Colaba's St Anne's School. Now she taught English language at Ontario's Blyth School, junior grade. In Mumbai, the Monteiros had led a balanced family life except for the dirt that couldn't be swept under the family's Moroccan carpet anymore. For years, Daniel was into serial affairs with his plays' leading ladies. Ignorance was bliss for Frances till Daniel's weekend trips with Bidisha, the stage-cum-TV actress, barely out of her teens, became front-page fodder for the tabloids.

Demanding commitment, she showed up one day at the Monteiros' upscale apartment on Marine Lines at an hour when the children were at school. Politically astute, she sobbed her heart out to her director's wife. The visit's effects, though, were salutary for Danny: one, the much-procrastinated plans to migrate to Canada went into fast track; two, Bidisha, never acted in theatre or TV again.

With time, her threats of a lawsuit died a natural death. No other director would touch her; she could embarrass them too, haul them to court. She spelt trouble.

Daniel escaped lightly; he always would. At 40, he was available for liaisons, no purse strings attached. All his earnings were for his family and mum's Bengalaru bills. He *did not* ensnare women. Every night of lovemaking was consensual, would always be. A gentleman in a tweed jacket and a linen shirt, he would not step out of turn. No flirting but if a desirable woman was to move her hand on his thigh, he wouldn't remove it. A man is a man is a man.

In any case, why feel guilty? After three kids, his wife was sexually switched off. She would not admit it but she was cold storage, he convinced himself. He could smell the dinner's prawn curry on her shapeless cotton maxi, so voluminous that half the intercourse involved undressing her. If Frances was motionless and suppressed a yawn, too bad, he was just partaking of his conjugal rights. If he hadn't, she wouldn't have liked that either. Distance was the ideal solution.

Daniel was extra-effusive with his brother-in-law in Ontario. He had what Daniel called 'influence'. Migration papers secured, the kids were thrilled, the wife was pleased, but did caution him, "Danny mind you, no hanky-panky while I am away. For a few months you can do without sex." She kissed him, ground her body against his and said as sexily as she could, "Come soon, will miss you...my tiger."

Paradox, paradox—she's begging for sex but doesn't want it. Frances is a confused wretch but then so is O Danny Boy.

The traffic's crazy. It's not good, not good for your clogged arteries but a man's got to do what he's got to do. Look Danny, it's your 12th play; it has to click big time. It's so Indian, rooted in the soil. Not one of those imitations of some fancy Broadway musicals. Here theatre legends are made once in a decade or two...and it helps if you've been in advertising, have the gift of the gab, sleep around... sorry, but then look who's talking?...so do you. Yeah Danny, what you lack is drive, cunning, a producer who's on the same page instead of the moron you've stuck with all over again. Shit, shit, shit.

Next time produce your play yourself, sell that goddamn piano at home for seed money...then yoohooo... you'll be a rock star. You'll grow a goatee if you must, pay for your hoardings, posters, bus-backs splashed all over town, south Mumbai at least. Theatre in the suburbs is too existential, meaningful and all that...but it's vital; that theatre is serious, inventive. Maybe some day you'll do an existential play, so don't knock it. You can be experimental Dan, Dan.

Yippee the traffic's moving. You should be at the rehearsals in another half-an-hour.

Screw it, stuck again. This traffic, this bloody mess, that's causing those nightmares...naah, they aren't that nasty...dreams, yeah weird dreams. Forget Aunty Thelma, you'll pray whatever comes to your heart.

Now come on, come clean. You're scared of dreaming again tonight. Maybe you can speak to Suresh, your Agony Aunt-Uncle ha ha. He'll tell you what you want to hear, "Danny, have a Scotch, watch porn and go to sleep." Don't need such advice, do you?

Those production guys at the rehearsal today had better fetch you brown bread chicken sandwiches. Healthy. If the bread's white, I'll bloody paint those sandwiches brown. Now now Danny, cool, be cool. Like your daughter says, "Coolio." The things these youngsters say nowadays. Hope she isn't dating some whitey in Ontario, I'll shoot her...aah this is it! The anxiety for those nightmares, naah dreams. What's in a dream? Hey jerk, get your carcass of a car moving. The light's green. *Can't you see, you...Your language, dear Danny. You're adorable. Or are you?*

The venue for the rehearsals, Adarsh Balak Vidyalaya, in a tossing and twisting back lane of Bandra, is used till 11 a.m. for pre-school children. It is painted an unusually cheerful yellow and green which never fails to calm Danny's nerves. The school's compound is a semi-circle of dark brown earth, cleared of stones. Daniel parks his car under the shade of a tree. Dilemma of the day: auditions for a lecherous patron of Mumbai's brothels. So far, all the candidates have been milk cakes, behaving like impotent dunderheads. "Come on get horny, get an erection," he had directed a veteran bit-player. The other artistes had tittered: boss was going through one of his bad sex days. The bit-player was affronted, "Sir, the girl is old enough to be my granddaughter. How can I get...you know..." Exactly! The hunt continued for the perfect debauch.

The production staff, in a tizzy about what the play was all about, lied, "We called many actors, Sir, no one is willing to play that...vulgar role."

Vulgar! That's it.

Exasperated, Daniel called up a Chandigarh actor to come down; he would be super for the role. Flattered, the actor paid for his airfare, signed up for the vulgar cameo for ten performances. He wouldn't get money but would be noticed by the Bollywood *badshahs* at the shows, *inshallah*. And the production was in the news; papers and magazines had reported extensively on *Road to Playhouse*, the red-light district of Mumbai since the Raj. It would be a break from conventional theatre.

Daniel didn't have any pretensions of being *artistic* but he wasn't willing to bung in the producer's request for anti-wife jibes, anti-woman punchlines. The director may be a swine in private; in public he wouldn't be associated with bedroom farces or stand-up comedies. Not his scene. He considered himself a notch above, so did the theatregoers and more crucially, the corporate sponsors. His plays were sophisticated, subtle, frequently a Neil Simon or Edward Albee camouflaged to the Indian upper middle-class context.

Over some two decades, he had directed 11 plays, all raking in profits for the producer. *Barefoot at Hanging Gardens* and *Who's Afraid of RK Narayan?* were sly send-offs on Simon and Albee. Deliciously funny in their irreverence for progressive American mores and Indian orthodoxy, they would be revived every year.

This time, Daniel had taken off more than he or anyone could chew perhaps: a look back at his childhood fascination with brothels on Grant Road's Playhouse *mohalla* mispronounced as Peela House by its inhabitants. Producer Samardeen Habib kept telling him to lighten the text. The five principal players kept grilling him about 'motivation' for every line of dialogue uttered. Daniel was being Zen. He had lost his temper a couple of times, almost spat on the bald pate of the producer. Then Zen some more.

The play's opening show was just five days away.

Dear dear Danny, you got it. It's this play stuff that's to blame for those horrifying red ocean dreams. What are you afraid of buddy? Road to Playhouse *will rock but Dan, don't ever make the mistake of hitching up with that Habib ever again. Just wants to make a quick buck. Nothing wrong with making money, but not like thiiiiiis! Paper flowers in the finale! Indeed! Come, come, get the rehearsals going. Smile, somewhat icily or your actors will get into that motivation number again.*

Rehearsals kicked off as soon as Daniel entered the Vidyalaya's classroom rented at a discounted rate initially for a month, which went on to become a year. Supporting players Anna Nayyar and Noor Merchant would steal the show. No doubt about that. Anna was portraying an ageing blind prostitute and Noor was playing her brother, loyal and loving to the end. It was the main character, the corrupt cop, that Daniel was worried about. This TV actor, Arjun Kalyanpur, couldn't act for nuts, and he had the audacity to ask for *motivation!* As for the leading lady, the prostitute's daughter who doesn't know about her antecedents, this new girl Sujata Rastogi, was good.

She needed to let go, she was holding herself back. Daniel was fond of her. He saw his daughter in her, wanted her to do well, chew up the scenery, become a star.

The script was complicated. The lighting designer couldn't tell lilac from pink (he liked pink, hell!). The sound guy was stone deaf. The production staff was either on the cell phone or sneaking cigarette breaks. The make-up guy had turned up with a box of dust resembling chilly powder. No brown bread sandwiches arrived at the rehearsal, of course. Still the show must go on.

Daniel gnashed his teeth, wondering if they would become powder some day.

Another desultory rehearsal over. Daniel had caught the production's cigarette fiend, whispering into his cell, "Rehearsals bad Sir. Too much time waste. And he's asking for brown bread again."

He kept a distance from his actors: Sujata was much too young and Anna way too old. He was an ideal professional, so he abstained from addressing the girls as "darling", "honey" and "you sexxxy thing, you."

The evening drive back to town wasn't excruciatingly painful. The Bandra-Worli sea link was heaven-sent. Daniel winged to the Willingdon Club. Booze companion, the happily unemployed Nestor D'Silva, was already drinking himself under the table. "Grnnn eveng," he slurred. "Bringgz usual for my frnnd Daah...nny." They were joined by Willy, sweating profusely after a calorie-burning regimen of swimming in the club's pool. Nestor,

Willy and Daniel had preferences in their poison: whisky, single malt and vodka respectively. Tanked up, two hours later the trio hopped over to the dining room for the buffet and another nightcap. Just another evening for the lads.

No domestic help, remote relative in the guest room, woman under the bed-sheets or pet dog waited for Danny at his apartment. No love, no affection. Daniel-playwright-director could die at this very moment, and it would be no big deal. His mother would show up with the wreath she was so nuts about.

At home, for the nth time Daniel R Monteiro flipped through the pages of Flaubert's *Madame Bovary* which sent him to a realm of dappled sunlight and velvet sensuality, as he downed the remains of a vodka bottle. He avoided the bed, cold and empty. No dreams today God, anything but that. Maybe, just maybe he could discuss his fear with Nestor at the Willingdon Club tomorrow. No way, Nestor's high as a fucking kite, don't want to fly with him. Perhaps he could call up Willy's psychoanalyst friend, Nandan Mitra. Not fair. Nandu never accepted money for lending his shoulder to any of the Willingdon boys. Perhaps Daniel could talk to Father Mendonca in the confession box but he didn't really have anything to confess: he's been a good boy, a sickeningly good boy.

Danny Danny, perhaps you should call up Frances. She will call you tigerrrrr; that will turn you on. Well, not really. Just relax, Danny boy. It's midnight plus...get into that bed right now. Sleep...deepsleep...

He woke up at 3 a.m. What, no dream? Great. He checked every hour. Nothing, half-asleep, half-awake. He was triumphant.

See you can control your mind. You said no dreams, and you've sailed through the night. Great, you're boss Danny boy. Love you. No shaving today. Think you'll let a beard sprout, get more distinguished, look like Hemingway. Women go for that. A little affair with Nestor's wife wouldn't be bad. She's such a tease, always touching your thigh; you'll let her feel your bloody post office next time.

The play premiered to a mixed response. One critic raved, "Brilliant, it raises the bar of theatre." Another carped, "Self-indulgent exercise in nostalgia." Yet another walked out in the intermission with his mistress, curling his thin lips to excrete, "Garbage."

The production fetched instant profits. Samardeen Habib splashed his own pictures on whichever page he could buy in the newspapers. Daniel's Bollywood acquaintances came to the show at his personal invitation; Habib saw to it that only he was featured, his arms flung around the shoulders of the Kapoors, Khans and Khannas.

Ten shows completed, the play was to travel to the UAE and the UK for the NRI audiences. "We can go to Ontario, of course," the producer winked, saying salaciously. "Must be missing your wife," and as an afterthought, added, "and kids."

Daniel took a silent oath at Sunday mass: he would produce his next play. He would write another original play, draw upon the personally experienced again. He would get cracking right away.

Daniel Monteiro sat at his desk for a week, a month, a year. The Microsoft Word doc on his computer screen remained blank. A clean slate. Return to Albee and Simon? Oh no, not done.

It wasn't that common-as-flu writer's block. It was something else...crimson oceans no longer opened up; yellow submarines had been swallowed up by an excess of reality; the dead were dead; the living still living...the Taj Mahal pristine white; the Gateway of India, sepia...

Daniel had lost his dreams.

Sunday Cognac Evenings

Vivan wasn't the typical aggressive reporter. In fact, the recruiting trainee manager of *The National Independent* had tried to talk him out of journalism: he was shy and overqualified which he was. The post-graduate would have worked on a PhD if he could have afforded the luxury. Subject: cinema on which he had been weaned by his doughty mother, her bank savings interest paying for the monthly household expenses and his education. Concurrently his awareness of world cinema had evolved with exposure to the French New Wave, Italian Neo-realism and a package of experimental short films from Germany's Oberhausen Festival. For a while he had suspended reading—at least two great classics a week and a bestseller paperback bunged in between—to become a movie junkie.

Vivan Ali's bio-data mentioned the co-editorship of *In Focus,* a film society magazine. Abbas Aagboatwalla was the co-hyphenate, a perceptive cineaste, who had additionally junked on crack and cocaine and willfully died of an overdose. Vivan continued to inject cinema in his veins but resolved to shun fanzine journalism which, to this day, means gossip. Tit bits, how prurient that sounds. Not his scene. The *In Focus* special issue on directors—exchanges with master filmmakers on their art and craft—had been a sell-out, a collector's item. If he pointed this out to anyone in mainstream journalism, the standard response was, "You've been out in the sun too long. Stop babbling. Nothing sinful about psst psssting. We all do it. We all love a bit of goss, don't we?"

"Yes, Sir."

He adapted. He could be a racy wordsmith and he could be cerebral in his deconstruction of cinema and celebrities of every genre and temperament. Vivan could be unashamedly devious while inveigling a star enigma to open up about the married man she adored. She would speak to him and no one else about her deranged obsession. He could see through her lies; she through his subterfuge techniques. She pretended to be nuts which she could well have been.

Now one day not quite certain whether he ought to be sly, clever or cerebral, Vivan Ali was en route to the highrise, Neptune Court, in the Juhu-Vile Parle scheme, Mumbai's *faux* Beverly Hills, to meet a thespian whom he had admired insanely ever since he could remember—his performances were astoundingly intense. How does this living legend—or something close to that—do it? The line separating the man from the actor was indistinct. It didn't matter to Vivan if younger actors had taken over the scene, outracing the thespian in popularity and market price. The intense artiste acted only in one film a year deluding the world that he was selective. Offers of any substance had dried up. Over 55, the actor was insecure but concealed that expertly. After much ado, an audience had been granted to *The National Independent* on a weekday, 2 p.m. The interview wouldn't have meant much if the legend had agreed immediately. True to convention, his secretary postponed and cancelled several meetings for over three months.

The interview was preceded by a formal phone call from the actor inquiring, "Will you share my humble lunch?" and then imploring, "No? Are you sure? Just some *daal, rotis*, green *salaaad.*" The extended pronunciation of salad rankled.

The actor wasn't sophisticated. He couldn't be: he had dropped out of a Hindi-Haryanvi school to run away to the city of cinema. He had spent years at a studio as a canteen waiter. On catching the eye of an ageing, terminally ill heroine, he nabbed that break every show business struggler prays for to a variety of gods in temples, mosques and churches. Someone would listen. The heroine, a former shadow of herself, after promoting the struggler passed away, it was said, in his arms. Next: her protégé lived hedonistically, entering and exiting from a series of make-up room liaisons with his heroines. Eventually acclaimed as a sensitive artiste, after a blitz of romantic roles, he was charm personified. At the height of his popularity, he courted and married a popular film playback singer. The divorce was quicker than the marriage. Before their first wedding anniversary, the spectacularly moody singer from a classical music *gharana*, made it public that she felt frustrated with the actor who symbolised romance. She couldn't be dependent on her husband financially, neither could she give up a career. Too bad if the actor saw her as a woman who must mind the home, raise children and live vacuously ever after. He did not see why his wife needed to spend hours with music composers, of dubious morals, at faraway sound recording studios. Not done. Permitting his wife—so far associated with music for connoisseurs—to resume her career and that too with a sleazy cabaret song, would have been irrational. Not done.

Vivan's taxi ride was taking an eternity to reach Neptune Court. Dismiss his private life stuff from your thatch, he had resolved. Zoom in on the professional. Nothing else matters...the film buff had wept copiously while watching his films. He had been shaken by the actor's artistry. Too much make-up perhaps but whenever the actor was photographed empathetically, he was God. Cinematographers can be hostile to actors who don't respect technicians. Ever since his debut, two cinematographers had endured his idiosyncrasies. Whenever he was lensed by them he was bathed in an angelic backlight, the crow's feet around his eyes and the double chins erased.

Vivan Ali would scoff when he interviewed neophyte actors. Dumb, dumb, they're so dumb. The thespian had to be a cut above; it would be such a pleasure to meet him. Pure joy. And what do you know? The artiste's secretary had requested a section of the interview to be quoted in a book—a collection of articles assembled by an acolyte chronicling the actor's *oeuvre*. The reporter-reviewer's byline carried weight. Or was it *The National Independent* that was quote-worthy?

"Honoured, please tell Sir I'm honoured." Quotes no problem.

In the waiting room of the Neptune Court home-cum-office, the fan was knobbed to maximum speed. Still Vivan was sweating, nervous. Don't. The man's human. He won't gobble you up. The legend lived on the upper section of the penthouse; the office, a row of rooms, was housed below. It was bereft of staff but for the secretary devoid of a distinctive face or personality. The automaton announced, "Sir will be with you shortly. Please be comfortable."

The actor had adopted a pseudonym gifted to him by his benefactress heroine. Born to a family of agriculturists in Narwana, Jind district, Humayun Din Muhammad went by the screen name of Aatish Kumar. It suited him—paradoxically—because he didn't live up to the sobriquet. He wasn't a flame, he wasn't fiery. He was tranquil, like his inner office room dominated by a life-size, blow-up of the benefactress who had passed away some 20 years ago.

Then there was a fawn leather swivel chair, white cushion, a grand black glass-topped desk holding a pile of books, a packet of extra-strong cigarettes, a gold lighter and monogrammed serviettes. Aatish Kumar arrived after 10 minutes—probably timed—wearing an afternoon beige cotton suit, not exactly in vogue, which albeit offset a ruddy complexion. He was clean shaven, pomaded and faintly perfumed.

He could have been Vivan's father. Perfection. Look at him. Look at him but don't gawk. Fathers are like that, smiling, kind compassionate, scrubbed, shaved. Too good to be true. Right then, Aatish offered the cigarette pack and lighter on the desk to Vivan, initiating the interview with, "Let's have tea and a cigarette. I am nervous of you."

An *abba* would *never* have asked a son to share a smoke.

The interviewer and his subject smoked cigarettes over weak tea. Vivan let the extra-strong dangle between his trembling fingers. Hope he didn't notice. He did, "You don't like the cigarette? Shall I order your brand for you?"

"No, Sir."

Trembles controlled, the interview proceeded desultorily. Ho ho hum. Aatish may be an outstanding actor but he was inarticulate and if a reply went beyond two of three lines it was pompous. Back at the news desk, Vivan didn't replay the answers on his dictaphone. Bored out of his skull, he typed the transcript yawning profusely. A quote, a sterile riff on Descartes, was reproduced in the Aatish collection, "I act, therefore I am."

The book was a blast of adulation; Vivan was embarrassed about his quote being featured in the collection. Wanly, he fielded a compliment when Aatish phoned to say, "That was an excellent piece...this non-entity doesn't deserve it. Your pen has some magic."

"Thank you, Sir."

"No, really," Aatish cartwheeled. "For once, I wasn't asked about my private life," and then abruptly he tossed the question, "Tell me, what are you doing this Sunday?

"Nothing, Sir," lied Vivan.

"I would be honoured if you shared a poor man's dinner at my humble abode."

Vivan thought, "No Sir, kind of you, Sir..." but said, "Sir, I would be honoured."

"What is your poison?"

"Whatever, Sir."

"*Wah!* Fine. I'll get a bottle or two of Whatever for us. Come at 7, please. I go to sleep by 10."

"Yes, Sir."

"You know my house? It's in..."

"I know, Sir. I have been there."

"But you must be going to so many places. I thought you might have forgotten. *Chaliye,* I don't want to take more of your valuable time. And please don't call me sir, *bache.*"

Bache? What's he saying?

"What should I call you, Sir?"

"How about *baba*?"

"Right, *baba*."

"*Chaliye,* Sunday it is...*ab Khuda haafiz bache*."

"Khuda haafiz...baba."

Sundays were reserved for his mother, Ameena Begum, a widow who wore white *lahenga-dupatta*s and a St-Joan-of-Arc-at-the-stake expression. She seldom discussed Vivan's father except when comparisons had to be drawn, "I thank Allah that you're not as irresponsible as your father. May his soul rest in peace. Eating any rubbish and then complaining of aches and pains till no doctor could save him." Ameena rarely moved out of the medium-sized home unless it was for an unavoidable visit to the dentist. A fanatic for black-and-white vintage films on Doordarshan, she infallibly rained invectives, "*Bakwas* story. And see the hero, he's thinner than a lizard. Oof, and that heroine is fatter than a shed of buffaloes. If they ever get married, they'll be a sight in bed."

Vivan imbibed her remarks gratefully, excluding the sexual innuendoes in his film reviews. This Sunday, he informed *ma,* "I have to go out for dinner."

"What!"

"It's work." And then he hit bull's eye, "My progress depends on this."

"Very well, then. I'll call Homai over. She presses my feet. Not like you. You don't love me. Work, work, work."

"I won't go, then."

"No, no, go. Your future is more important. Just tell that Homai to come over."

Homai Agha, their spinster neighbour ever the willing mummy-sitter, agreed. She had time on her hand. Besides, she looked upon Ameena Begum as a surrogate mother.

Surrogate, so dangerous when the limits are crossed.

Vivan was touchy about the surrogacy factor. Before turning 30, he had idealised at least three men as his absent father: a neighbourhood businessman, a friend's father, and a celebrity film scriptwriter who would drop by at his apartment to repeatedly reassure *ma*, "Don't worry, when you're gone, I'll take care of him."

"Promise me, that you'll never let go of his hand. You're a good man. He needs a father like you," *ma* would get maudlin.

Subsequently when Vivan criticised the film writer's Hollywood-plagiarised script, saying in no uncertain words that the dialogue stank, the good man dropped Vivan the way he would drop a bad habit. All contact lines were severed the morning the review appeared in print.

"He used to be so good to us," *ma* would miss him. "Did you two quarrel? You shouldn't. You never know when you'll need him."

"That's it...this film world is need-based. Forget him."

"*Lo,* forgotten. Now you'll be with me on Sundays again. That's enough for me."

"Yes, if my work permits."

The first surrogate *abba,* the businessman, his wife and kids, stayed in an adjoining upscale housing complex. The Sanghvis were all smiles, included him in their festival lunches and ceremonies till one day, he was left out of a *havan.* Businessman Bhupendra Sanghvi told him casually, "You will not know anyone...you will get fed up sitting there," but Vivan understood that he would be the only Muslim and that would make Mrs Sanghvi feel awkward.

As for the friend's father, documentary filmmaker Deven Mukherjee, he passed away prematurely. Mukherjee's heart seizure had been precipitated by hypertension, which no one had perceived, least of all his son who said at the funeral, "I think dad liked you more than he cared for me. Must be because of your writing. You media people have some special bond or what? He did not like me much; we had our differences. I could not understand his dreary documentaries."

Vivan missed Mukherjee but only when he passed by his apartment to which he was no longer invited for Sunday brunches.

Now a Sunday profession-enhancing dinner with the thespian was on the menu; the blade-sharp mother said, "*Beta,* I hope you're going to office and nowhere else. I know you haven't forgotten that *haraamzada* film writer. Really you shouldn't have criticised his script. No one can take criticism...can you? Anyway you know best."

Vivan had forgotten but not forgiven. The scriptwriter, the businessman's family and the documentary filmmaker's son had violated him emotionally. He had allowed them to. Careful, baby, careful; easier thought than done.

One Sunday evening at the Neptune Court penthouse dissolved into another. Vivan was given access to the top residential storey, marble-floored, tastefully decorated with prints of old-age Britain landscape paintings. Dinners were preceded by conversation on corrupt political leaders, the deteriorating standard of cinema and showbiz gossip. The duologues were accompanied by VSOP cognac, bottles removed from a wall cupboard, for guests who appreciated the finer things of life. And of course, there was only one guest at this point of the actor's life and times, who had refinement and taste.

VSOP-warmed, Vivan would pat Lakhan, Aatish Kumar's Labrador. Intermittently Vivan sketched his own life story. Aatish didn't patronise his guest, expressed his sympathies for Vivan left fatherless at the age of five. "I am here for you always. See you next Sunday. I want to know more," Aatish said sombrely.

"No *baba,* not Sunday."

"Any day. This house is yours."

Reporter, journalist, reviewer, interviewer, snoop, tinker, tailor, he didn't know who he was at those Sunday dinners. He wasn't stimulated intellectually at all but come on, unwind, there was a sense of belonging.

After the first dinner, Vivan had been escorted to the waiting taxi. Aatish had closed the door gently, and placed his hand on his heart to say, "Good night, thank you for your company, *dil-o-jaan se*." The midnight-weary driver was instructed, "Drive carefully, your passenger is precious."

Oh oh, not again. Be vigilant...don't get fond of this man. Vivan had wailed on losing his previous surrogates. Stories, stories, so many stories abound in love, heartache, romance. His stories were of mourning the loss of dads and of lasting scars. They were all alike. Aatish was vain too, peacock proud, bristling at the showbiz swines who had not financed any of his films when he had expressed the desire to turn to direction. He had written poems in Urduish, painted on Sunday mornings. He considered himself a far superior actor to the other Kumars and Khanna-come-lately. He wasn't on Sunset Boulevard, far from it, but wouldn't admit that the route was a possibility.

His estranged wife Radhika—greying exquisitely—who was back on the hit parade, fetched up on a Sunday evening. She looked pointedly at Aatish and Vivan, and carped, "Superb! Superbbbbb! What would life be without drinking companions?" Turning to Aatish, she said spitefully, "I hear you still want to become a director. Please don't. You're only good at acting, and you know it."

"At least you admit that I'm a good actor, dearest."

"Don't *dearest* me. You're a good actor when you don't ham."

"When did I ham?"

"Never mind," she said curtly. "I won't embarrass you before your friend. Go ahead, drink, drink. Cheers boys!"

She helped herself to a soda and ice.

Aatish grinned, "Still pretending, still pretending. Have a drink *yaar.* Cognac *chalega*? Don't worry, Vivan is family. He won't write that you drink."

Radhika countered, "Ask me if I care if he writes or doesn't write! He seems to praise only you nowadays. I don't feel like a drink today. That's all."

The estranged couple bantered. Radhika knocked down a couple of sherries. At one point, the couple almost came to blows. Vivan tried to flee. Neither would let him. After all, he was family. Vivan and Aatish had met at a juncture when one was down, the other blooming. Perhaps Vivan was attracted by the actor's aloneness. He didn't like bunking the Sunday dinners at Neptune Court but attempted to stay away occasionally, in vain.

"Sundays with you are so calm," Aatish said airily. "I can call someone else over but I am so used to you... *bache* you're a bad habit."

"Sundays are the only time I get with *ma.* It's been ages...I should be with her this Sunday. She's not feeling too well."

"Alright, as you wish," the actor responded over the phone. Dead silence.

"But maybe I'll drop by."

"Maybe is neither here nor there."

"I'll be there."

"Not here?" Aatish warmed up.

"I'll leave a bit early."

"Then you come a bit early"

"Yes, Sir."

"What do you mean, Sir?"

"Yes *baba*."

Vivan was neither naïve nor entirely selfless. He was feeding off the thespian's dinners. He was learning so much about the Mumbai film industry from his witty anecdotes. He was wanted, that too by a childhood hero superior to the New Age wooden actors. So oak, so teak. Vivan's ego was boosted; he was being regarded as a son, an equal, an 'intellectual'.

Jangling, that. Vivan Ali was no intellectual. At most he was whip-smart and crafty. He could distinguish an 'I' from a 'Q'. If Aatish had not allocated an upper berth to him in that penthouse, he would have been devastated. Vivan had found an admirer; the admiration was reciprocated abundantly.

For over three years, they were inseparable. One had to know where the other went, did, slept, ate. They would even talk to each about their bowel movements. "I took long in the bathroom today, *bache*. That's why I couldn't call you before breakfast. My—what do you *angreziwalla*s call it?—tummy is making sound today," Aatish would inform the all-ears Vivan. Two phone calls a day were mandatory. Their friendship was talked about, envied.

An upcoming actor, who had wangled himself an invitation to the Neptune Court penthouse, did not like what he saw on a Sunday evening. Vivan's glass of cognac was being refilled, the platters of *kabab*s re-re-offered to him rather than to Upcoming or his aspiring fashion designer fiancée. Jealousy mounting, Upcoming downed three or four too many from the bottle which hadn't been offered to him. Upcoming sought undivided attention. Banging his forehead hard and repeatedly on the carpet, he wept, "Why? Why? Why do you favour this...this bloody journalist? "

Head-banger Upcoming's fiancée watched on with alarm. Aatish didn't move from his customary lazy chair. Vivan reversed gear, taxied home, amused and wickedly victorious, "What a fool. Tomorrow he will have a bump on his forehead. Of course, *baba* loves me more than him." He crept into his bedroom. *Ma* was asleep, no need for breath-camouflaging *elaichi*s today. That callow actor, what's wrong with him? What a dolt!

Next morning, Aatish phoned to ask with mock innocence, "What made you leave so early?"

"Just, it was very late."

"Nothing else *bache*?"

"Nothing."

"Good, I was afraid that you might be upset."

"Not at all, *baba*."

"What are you doing just now?"

"Talking to you."

"I know that. Now you're talking like your *baba*... *barkhurdar*, it is your Radhika *didi's* birthday tomorrow. We are all going out for dinner."

"I'll be there. *Didi?* Can I call her that?

"Of course, she is very fond of you. I will let you know the time and place."

"Yes, *baba*."

At the Chinese resto-disco, *didi* and Vivan danced to the Bee Gees. "Night fever, night fever." They flayed arms and limbs to "Killing me softly". Aatish gawked with disco eyes, "*Shabash*, I didn't know you could dance, I liked seeing you happy *bache*."

Vivan was floored. Someone cared, loved him...*night fever night fever*. Sunday *durbars* became Saturday-Sunday *durbars*. Aatish whipped out a $100 note when Vivan had to fly overnight to Venice for an assignment: "Every time you go abroad, you'll get $100. Get me a cognac, the rest you spend...*beta*." Like the thespian's pet, Lakhan, Vivan wagged his tail.

This surrogate father wasn't like the others; they belonged to each other. Aatish was possessive about him; Vivan pretended he wasn't possessive about his ersatz dad. Despite his graceful Urdu diction and disposition, Aatish suffered from what could be termed an inferiority complex. He wasn't fluent in English. Vivan corrected his pronunciations, ghost authored articles for him—with a hidden agenda. His byline carried weight since B-towners didn't ever write signed pieces in the papers...

or more accurately, couldn't. In turn, Aatish would be congratulated by his golf course cronies for his series of articles on topics ranging from the city's civic issues to nostalgia-plated reminiscences.

For the death anniversary of the benefactress heroine, preserved in that larger-than-life blow-up, Vivan titled the thespian's chaotically dictated tribute, "Beautiful Loser", a snitch from Leonard Cohen since newspaper headlines aren't copyright bound. Aatish was blitzed with compliments, "What a poetic title."

To congratulate themselves for the widely praised "Beautiful Loser", Vivan and Aatish planned a Sunday evening at the new Italian resto-bar in town.

"*Yeh pasta-vasta.* Spaghetti, you teach me how to eat. It's like eating a woman's hair."

"Yes, *baba.*"

"And what's Chianti wine? Expensive?"

Dinners, lunches, breakfasts...Vivan had found a home, perhaps even an idol. Separately they were invited to a film festival in London. Aatish Kumar said petulantly, "If you're going, I will. Or else, I will be a pomfret out of water! You'll *sambhalo* my English."

The idol and his pet were like schoolgirls on Leicester Square, going tee-hee-hee over three-scoop ice-creams tubs and almond-flaked brownies. Aatish assured Vivan, "Don't worry about foreign exchange. This one's on me."

"No, no. I'll pay you back in rupees in Mumbai."

"Shut up! Today, let's try out Lebanese cuisine, then walk *karte hain.* Let's see what this great Thames is about."

Walking till 4 a.m., teeth chattering in the cold, sharing a paper cone of roasted chestnuts...Vivan was on top of the Big Ben. "Dad, dad, dad...may I embrace you please?" he yearned to say but couldn't. The built-in warning buzzed, "Hang on, you're a professional. Keep that distance. Quit accepting the freebies. What if you roast his performance some day? You'll be sacked, in the manner of a domestic help, to be replaced instantly. Or more accurately, exiled to another kennel like Lakhan the Labrador if he ever dared to bite...or bark. That head-banger actor is waiting to take over, isn't he? Hey, but stop being so uptight. *Baba* cares for you. You adore him."

Baba had just left for Coventry and then on to Hounslow, to feature in a round of Asian Radio chat shows. Vivan was left alone in an Oxford Circus hotel room. *Baba* would be back in two days. He could have gone along but chose not to hang around him. He would rather see London. As soon as the actor left in a stretch limo, Vivan missed him so much, it ached. He couldn't watch the comedy shows on television; he couldn't read a book. And he hated the view of the Thames from the hotel window, "Looks like a gutter."

The phone rang, "*Bache,* are you alright? Did you go to Tussaud's? Windsor Manor? Kew Gardens? *Kyoon nahin?* This English language *bhi na?* Too much Kew Kew. You missing me?"

"Yes *baba*."

"I wanted to ask you for something, if you don't mind."

"Yes *baba*, tell me."

"Can you organise £800 here? I need the money... only if you can, Puchku."

Puchku? Lovely.

"Yes, Sir."

"*Sir ka bacha*. Where will you get it?"

Vivan cadged the pounds from the family of Naveen, a schoolfriend settled in Belgravia, chip chip, jolly fancy. Naveen's mother had a soft corner for Vivan: her boorish son had graduated after copying Vivan's constitutional history answer sheet. Naveen was travelling but that's okay. Unintentionally rude though, Mother Belgravia said with a flourish on handing over the money, "This is for all the help you've given my son. You don't have to pay it back. Spend it well. Take something for your mother... how is she? The silk flowers at Harrods' are lovely."

Eight hundred pounds were handed over to Aatish who shoved them into his tweed jacket's pocket, then rubbed Vivan's cheek sweetly. Vivan wouldn't be able to buy silk roses for *ma*, but he *had* whisked away the in-flight blanket on British Airways. She would love it, plus maybe he could pick up some duty-free chocolates, a box of candy. She would pop an éclair in her mouth, pretend to be a child and lisp, "Can I have one more please?"

Ma no one compares to you.

This man Aatish Kumar was selfish. What did he need those £800 for? He could have got them from anywhere. The shame that had to be endured—£ 800 for a friend's graduation fee. "Vivan, Vivan, take it easy. DON'T REACT," he kept chanting as if it were a prayer.

Back in Mumbai, Sundays reverted rhythmically to the beat of Aatish *baba,* Lakhan the Labrador, cognacs and *kababs*. Then Vivan was off again—Los Angeles, *Ellay* if you please in the actor's pun-speak. He was on an MTV junket to report on Madonna *'live'*. Aatish didn't approve, "You're too intelligent to run after pop girls." *Intelligent,* he had said this time, *not intellectual*. Relief. But no $ 100 for LA. The promise had been forgotten. Forget it, forget it, FORGET IT.

Vivan returned from *Ellay,* loaded with gifts, more for his *ma* than for *baba*. He bought an expensive Cartier lighter for Aatish *baba,* who remonstrated, "You want me to smoke more and die of cancer? Your gift should have been more thoughtful. I'm old enough to be your father. Would you give him a lighter? What did you get your mother?"

"A cordless phone, chocolates, a Hermès scarf, crystal, silk flowers."

"I would have preferred chocolates or silk flowers to this," Aatish tossed the lighter into a drawer next to his lazy chair, slamming it shut.

"I'll get some of the chocolates and silk flowers from *ma*."

"No second-hand presents. Anyway, it's late now. You'll find a taxi on the road."

Aatish Kumar didn't escort him to the taxi. No sound of the door closing. Vivan wept soundlessly, slapping himself with words, "I don't ever learn, I don't ever learn. Cut this man out of your system now, he is meanmeanmean."

For a week whenever the phone rang, it wasn't Aatish *baba*. If cell phones existed then, Vivan would have placed his on silent mode. He couldn't bear the thought of answering a call with that paternal voice at the other end. Yet, he wanted him to call. It was an hour-by-hour agony, then minute by minute. Aatish *baba* was probably delivering one of his best performances.

Aatish didn't call. Vivan wouldn't call.

Ameena *ma* didn't notice any change in her boy; he just seemed to be writing away more furiously, at a distance. She couldn't tell that he was covering pages and pages with the three words—Enough is enough, Enough is enough, Enough is enough, Enough is enough.

Vivan went through the drill again, speaking to himself silently, "You imbecile, he isn't your daddy. You won't ever find a surrogate dad, so grow up, grow up, grow up." He would slide his head on *ma*'s lap while she watched TV. She wasn't demonstrative, and would shoo him away, "It's so warm. Take your face away, go do something, write."

Enough is enough, Enough is enough.

It never is.

Silence is a lethal weapon.

Distraught, Vivan tossed and turned in bed. Close to 1 a.m., he picked up the cordless and dialled Radhika *didi.*

"Hello, *didi,*" he said. No need to lower his voice. *Ma* slept as soundly as a baby.

"Hello? What happened? You want to go the disco? It must be shut." Joke.

"*Didi, baba* has been behaving strangely."

"Oh," a peal of laughter, then "You just realised. Better late than never."

"Why?"

"He can't take anyone after a point of time. Short attention span. Low tolerance level, *jo bhi hai.* I knew this would happen."

"That's not fair."

"So who said life is fair? Listen, you will always be welcome to my house. I am your *didi.* Get away from him."

"I have to. Enough is enough."

"Then promise me that you will not go back."

"I will not go back."

"Let's see."

"*Didi,* if you don't mind, may I ask you something?"

"Go ahead. You journalists have nothing but questions in your head."

"*Didi,* why do you keep going back to him? Visiting him?"

"You idiot, I was his wife. You aren't."

"What are you saying, *didi*?"

"Get smart. He needed you, you've given him more media exposure than he deserves in this lifetime. *Bahut ho gaya.* He doesn't need you now.You are not his son. You cannot be."

"I know that."

"Good. Now go to sleep."

"Thank you, *didi.*"

"Don't go back, don't call him. It won't make any difference to him. Good night."

That man cared a damn for him. End, end it now. It could have been worse. It was.

As soon as he heard early morning sounds, which he didn't ordinarily, he called Aatish, an early riser, "*Baba,* how are you?"

"How do you think? I don't like the way you are behaving. You know I care for you like my own son. Come over this evening. Don't be late."

Vivan danced wildly before the mirror. *Baba* cared. At the news desk, he wrote up an editorial on the deteriorating state of cinema which was so incisive that news editor Shripati Rao beamed, "That's my boy! You write serious stuff with spice."

Nirvana was near.

That evening Aatish Kumar lit an extra-strong with the Cartier, and said, "This must be expensive. Thank you, *bache.* I was in a bad mood, I took it out on you...you should know me better." Reassuringly, the actor hadn't removed a framed photograph with the journalist.

It was still there, lodged prominently among family memorabilia. *Didi* and *baba, bacha* and *baba*. Swoon. Vivan would never suffer again. Nevernevernever.

That night, after cognac and dinner, *baba* closed the taxi door shut, instructing the cabby, "Drive carefully. Your passenger is very precious."

❧

Life was splendid, marvellous, beouutiful. Vivan's heart resumed its beat. There was no quantity like enough. Enough is enough is enough. So childish in retrospect. Aatish *baba* was his, and to think he had almost lost him. Whenever he could, which was often, the journalist composed print paeans for the actor. He also influenced a jury to award the actor for a performance that was at best middling. Vivan suppressed his second thoughts. "That piece of performance was quite overwrought," he admitted to *ma*. "So what? All the actors in competition for the best supporting actor were over-the-top. *Baba*'s performance was the best of a terrible lot."

"I don't agree with you," *ma* responded. "I just hope you know what you are doing. You have been unethical. If I interfere, it'll only make matters worse. Some days, I feel like calling up that Aatish*baaz* of yours and warning him to leave you alone."

Vivan ignored her threat. He psyched himself. *Baba* needed the trophy; it looks terrific standing next to the dozens he had won during his heyday. Several Sundays the thespian had pointed a finger at the crowded mantelpiece, and said morosely, "Those trophies must be longing for some new company."

The Sunday after the awards function, *didi* dropped by at Nepturne Court. One look at Vivan, and she said, "No hope for you."

"What do you mean no hope?" *Baba* Aatish asked.

"Why must you know everything? This is between Vivan and me."

"*Oho,* your *didi* loves you."

"You don't know the meaning of love, never did."

"Shut up," he snapped.

Vivan butted in, "*Didi,* I heard you're recording a solo album of love songs soon."

Aatish sniped, "Love? Don't make me laugh."

Didi retaliated, "You will laugh the day I win an award which is deserved.What are you winning nowadays Aatish *saab*? Awards from boys you corrupt with cognac?"

Very uncharacteristically, Vivan took that calmly: Radhika *didi* didn't mean what she said, she was in one of her moods. He suggested genially,"No fighting please."

Baba agreed, "Tell your *didi,* not me."

"Tell your *baba,* not me."

"*Baba,* don't."

"If you say so," Aatish conceded. "Then I have to agree."

"Peace, peace, peace."

"Peace *pullao* is cooking for dinner today or what?" Aatish punned, waiting for appreciative chortles.

"You've murdered many things," *Didi* clucked. "Leave the English language in peace."

"That's what I said, peas."

Then a U-turn by *didi,* "I had brought some baked chicken. Have it if you like...or throw it away," and left.

Aatish Kumar and Radhika were made for each other but their egos wouldn't accept that. Maybe some day Vivan could bring them together, they could remarry. *Baba* and *didi* under the same roof...paradiso regained.

During the taxi ride home that night Vivan felt like an angel about to grow wings. He'd do that? Play Cupid. Naah, forget it, they were incompatible. No butting in Vivan, stay within limits.

Vivan's friend Anand Marwah, a professor of cinema, warned him, "You're conscious about the fact that there can be no susbtitute father. Yet you keep promoting that has-been. Be careful. You're chasing illusions."

All friends had been placed on hold for the actor. No one else mattered; he didn't want to be with anyone in the whole wide world but Aatish *baba.* If Vivan was gifting *baba* books, Hermès neckties, a Vuitton bag, and whatever else he could just about afford, he was being showered with love. That sense of belonging was priceless, it even made him excel at his work. He was promoted every six months, salary hiked.

Ameena *ma* was content. That actor fellow hadn't damaged her boy's feelings. Indeed, her son had struck a balance. He had matured, a responsible professional, ostensibly emotionally grounded too.

News editor Shripati Rao and Vivan would go out for a beer session mid-week, his boss on his fifth, the journalist on his sixth lager. "You can hold your beers," Rao noted. "You've become a respectable journalist."

A yearly seminar on cinema in Calcutta was just round the corner. Vivan was to cover the event for his newspaper. Doordarshan commissioned the journalist to interview *the names,* national and international. Aatish was one of them, expounding on the limitations in the realm of film acting. Location—the Grand Hotel suite where the official delegates were housed.

"Don't ask me silly questions *bache,*" Aatish suggested, his smile marshmallow soft. "You know I'm doing the interview just for you."

"How can I ask you silly questions?" the *faux* son said, dressed for the occasion in a designer Jodhpuri.

"You're looking very handsome," Aatish said studying the interviewer.

"Am I?"

"I wouldn't say so if I didn't mean that. You're a handsome *bacha.*"

The interview—like his first—was a disaster. The journalist aiming at objectivity, initiated the conversation with, "You seem to be a misogynist. You hardly seem to have any chemistry with your heroines."

The actor called for a halt, "I will not dignify that question with an answer."

The TV crew gasped. Cursing himself for the politically incorrect starter, Vivan switched to bubble-gum questions.

Predictable questions, predictable answers.

At the end of an hour, Aatish Kumar was aglow. The taped interview would be telecast at 9.30 pm, in the prime slot, after the daily news bulletin.

Cognac carried to Calcutta from the wall cupboard, *kababs* and *salaaads* from room service were spread out on the coffee table of the actor's suite. "They always reserve this suite for me," the thespian crowed. "In Calcutta, I wouldn't dream of staying anywhere else." After Vivan's clearance, the actor had invited Anirudh Roy, a crusty old singer known as the Bard of Bengal, his housemaker wife, and a movie starlet. Vivan had noticed the starlet slinking that afternoon into the greenhouse of Eastern Hotel with a middle-aged, married media honcho. This woman ensnared men effortlessy. A sexual dalliance was as natural to her as her killer lips. She didn't conceal her sexuality. It should be a fun evening. If she was in the suite tonight, at least there would be some conversational chemistry.

Starlet Veena Sharma was drinking greedily. The bard rendered his version of a protest from the days of the struggle against the British Raj. His wife chipped in, "Anirudh, when you sing, my tears flow...like a river."

Eeesh.

Aatish chain-smoked and said seriously, "I'm nervous to see my TV interview. This boy asked me some really silly questions."

"Can't be," the bard swigged a rum-and-cola. "He is too sensible."

"Isn't he looking handsome today?" Veena piped in, exhaling a cirrus cloud from a mint cigarillo. "Only trouble is that he doesn't ever look at me."

"Come on Veena, he has always told me that he likes you. He's a bit shy, that's all," Aatish fibbed.

The Doordarshan interview was on. Mediocre: a giddy-headed fan chirruping in agreement to the actor's bland statements. When Aatish said, "I worship women in real and in reel life. I place them on a pedestal...you should know that," Vivan winced in view of the TV camera, and again in the suite.

The gathering raised a toast to the interview, to Vivan who was looking so very handsome. Anirudh Roy asked smarmily, "How come you've never interviewed me? You ask such intellectual questions."

"Oh shut up. All of you are pathetic!" Vivan suppressed a scream. He needed *baba,* that's all. So what if this dad or whatever he is happens to be nothing but a poseur, a hypocrite? No one's perfect.

A dessert spread was served by a waiter who left without a tip. On the grounds of some half-baked principle, Aatish did not tip, "They charge so much. This tax, that tax. Imagine ₹ 500 for a caramel custard," he explained, aware that Vivan wasn't thrilled with his hotel dining etiquette.

"Why aren't you having dessert young man?" the bard inquired. "On a diet or what?"

Eeesh.

"Just tired," Vivan murmured.

"*Aah* but then you don't need caramel," the bard's wife spoke her last line of the evening. "You're so sweet."

"Yes, we should have him for dessert," Veena laughed at her own insinuation.

Midnight. It was way past Aatish *baba's* bedtime.

Vivan marshalled the starlet, bard and wife, "Let's go. *Baba* needs to sleep."

"See how much he cares for you," the bard remarked. "Vivan, we will drop you at your hotel. We will have the privilege of your intellectual company."

Eeesh.

"It will be a detour for you. I'll take a taxi," Vivan said instinctively, "Veena, aren't you at the Eastern Hotel also?"

"Yes. But I'll take a taxi later. You all go ahead."

"Now, now, you girls fuss too much," the bard addressed the starlet. "There's enough room in the car for the four of us."

Aatish resembled the Sphinx. He didn't say a word.

To escape the suite, Vivan thanked the bard, "That's very kind of you. Let's go."

The bard, his wife and Vivan trooped out of the suite, inching towards the elevator. Veena didn't budge.

"Veena, come on, it's very late," Vivan called out.

"I'm spending the night here. Do you mind?"

"What?"

"You mind?"

Aatish Sphinxed some more. Vivan made eye contact. Not a flicker of an expression which could be decoded. "Go *bache*," he said "See you in the morning."

The actor closed the suite's door on Vivan who suspended thought. Don't think, just go, GO.

It couldn't be...it couldn't be what he was thinking.

At the Eastern Hotel, oddly enoughVivan slept soundly. On waking up, he began shaving, avoided the reflection in the mirror, when he heard himself say, "You hate him, you hate him. He's just like all the others. You've wounded yourself again, damn it again. You thought he is your idol. And see this idol turns out to have clay feet. What a corny metaphor! *Enough is enough is enough*. You're possessive, so what? Every normal human being would be possessive in your situation. You hate him...such a worm, the way he shut the door on you. He must have slept with her all night long. Wonder how many times they did it. Good for him, great. But would you have let your real dad do that? Anyway, anyway...fuck it...get out of this pit. These guys have no morals, no honesty...the bloody bitch...the way she stared at me, taunting me. But why are you so upset? Let him sleep around. So what? OH SHUT UP."

Aatish Kumar and Veena Sharma walked up to him at the seminar venue jauntily, just short of being arm-in-arm. Aatish inquired with concern, "*Bache,* did you sleep well?"

Veena didn't say a word.

Vivan had to say it, taking care to omit the *baba* word, " You know what? Just fuck off."

And then he walked away. He didn't look back, released from an emotional cage. He felt better, so much better. Sundays with *ma,* back with his buddies, a beer or two with Shripati Rao, no cognacs, never never.

Back to the breathe-easy beat.

On his 32nd birthday, *didi* sent the journalist a bunch of silver-papered balloons, a carton of candy and a note: "Happy birthday. You're a big boy now. Get a life."

Vivan did. A decade later at 42, he was wearing his first pair of spectacles. Short-sighted but his career was on a cushy plateau. Meanwhile Aatish Kumar had made a comeback with a series of box office successes. He had stopped pretending that he was selective. Grabbed every offer he received.

That Sunday evening, *baba* was inaugurating an exhibition of abstract paintings.

Sighting him in the crowd, Vivan Ali rushed to Aatish Kumar, his heart beating wildly, "Sir, *baba,* how are you? Remember me?"

"No."

The Resignation Letter

He can detect the brand of cigarettes on a smoker's breath—lite, strong, filter tipped, not tipped, international, national, tobacco from Virginia packed in a factory here. He can predict the Mohammed Rafi-Kishore Kumar oldies which will be broadcast by the deejay of Radio Khichdi during the morning taxi ride from the Lokhandwala complex down the highways to his centre-town newspaper office, its walls jaundiced. The dumb-dumb deejay will call the songs of love and remorse, 'golden oldies'. The entertainment supplement editor—euphemistically called the Arts Editor—can forecast the intervening ad jingles of the day's drive. He can mimic every syllable of the contest offers, the chat-ups with celebrities who sound just like their Cave Age ancestors did: *I love my work...I am looking forward to my next release...it was a challenging role...I am learning every new day...*

Auushaddup.

Imtiaz Ashraf Ali, senior journalist, can forecast tomorrow's temperatures more accurately than the weather-beaten bureau. He can use inductive *and* deductive logic on body language. He can tell if that executive with the briefcase crossing the road to the Dadar overbridge had sex the night before or just an hour ago. When he says casually to a colleague sharing the ride, "That chap did it but that fellow...there...standing at the bus-stop...yeah in the striped shirt, didn't," he draws polite chuckles and also behind-the-back-sniggers.

He's strange. He can read thought bubbles, and startles the soapy office receptionist, "You hate the shirt I am wearing. Too dull. You get me a new one, ha ha."

The girl, in the ketchup T-shirt, reacts, "How did you know, Sir? I will get you a cool shirt for your birthday." More ha-ha-has.

"Er...when is the birthday?" she asks. He pretends not to hear.

He can walk past his most industrious reporter, squelching him, "You missed the story—that Rishabh Khanna is staying in a Marriott suite. His wife threw him out of the house. He's been having it on with that...what's her name? You should have made the calls I'd asked you to."

Library-soft silence follows.

Today Imtiaz suspects that he will leave the jaundiced office forever. No more Rishabh Khanna-starlet liaisons to immortalise. Such relief. He reads the water on his desk...it lacks transparency. He suppresses his anxiety; his intuition could be wrong. No, not today. He has planned to quit three months later in the merry month of May, merry because he was born in May, an event he celebrates with a cake. He buys it from a hotel's bakery the previous evening, cuts it in the morning, devours a slice and hands over the rest to the next-door-neighbour, the Kapoors, who never fail to ask, "Oh, is it your birthday?" He denies that every year. They don't really want to know anyway.

That eel of anxiety, it's slippery. He came to this newspaper group because there was none other left, none big enough for his boots. Twenty-seven years he had spent with another media group, entering as a cub still to sprout whiskers. His career: an athletic beginning, a flabby middle and now the finale, scrawny as his physical frame today, illnesses-ravaged. Allergies hum if the air-conditioner's temperature rises above 20°C. Cholesterol forbids red meat...borderline sugar prevents sugar. X-rays reveal stress in the lumbar region...a night attack of uric acid leaves him blinking like a neon sign out of order. Still he has hidden his transient limp, his back stabs and miscellaneous aches...these too shall pass.

Never missed a day's work. Bouts of self-congratulation. If they were to feed the attendance data of the staff in a computer, he would emerge as *Mr National Focus*. Mr Perfect. Runners-up? Naah, far far away.

There will be an intercom buzz today, he senses. An appointment with that porpoise-like HR executive (HR...human *resources*, ahem). The bloke, who empties an entire bottle of crow-black dye on his straggly hair, has arrived from the flagship office in New Delhi by the early morning flight. Kewal C Mishra, MBA, makes frequent trips to Mumbai, far too frequent and long-drawn-out, enticing rumours that he leads a double life. Travels business class, thanks to the corporate scheme of discount coupons, eventually working out cheaper than the much Tharoor-tweeted cattle class.

At this very minute, Imtiaz's secretary, the back-from-retirement VK Kutty, whizzes past the Arts Editor's cabin, wrinkled wooden doors left open; the air-conditioner is misbehaving again.

Imtiaz edits a rag, the daily newspaper's glam handmaiden, *NF Fundoo*. The name was finalised two years ago over such options as *NF Factor, NF Parade, NF Masala*. He has dumbed himself down. No no, he hasn't. He wouldn't do that, *never ever*. Not entirely sure. He opposed the exclusion of columns devoted to theatre, books and art. Didn't work; pages carrying such heavy-duty columns are denied ads. Loud and booming, he was told by the media group's owner that theatre and art are elitist; books are being downloaded. "Personally, I'm very fond of books," the group's owner had declaimed. "Paulo Coelho has changed my life." Now that's alchemistry. To each his own.

Imtiaz is into Thomas Mann, John Berger and of late JM Coetzee but Roland Barthes confounds him. And the historian DD Kosambi...Imtiaz packs up after the first chapter. After all these years of slogging, he is Arts Editor. He would like to think that he is the coolest in the business simply because there is no competition. Still, intellectual he's not, he laments repeatedly to himself, whenever a movie director or cleavage-popping startlet flatters him, "You're an intellectual unlike us...we merely want entertainment at the movies." *Take a walk guys.*

Gen-Next is Gen-Nix. Some years ago—2000 actually—a particularly distasteful gnome, a reporter with hair spiked like barbed wire, hacked into his Gmail account, and circulated Imtiaz's correspondence with a friend on confronting the death of the only woman he has ever loved—his mother.

Gnome's colleagues informed Imtiaz about it. But Gnome got away with that, the management being either abjectly indifferent or closet mother-bashers.

Then there was the duplicitous, syrupy-slimy Tubby who entered Imtiaz's room one day, plonked C-grade interviews with B-grade actors as his claims to fame, subsequently imitated his writing style to the Tee-hee but was patently mediocre if not third-rate. Tubby wanted to be as "intellectual" as Imtiaz, without knowing the *cee* of cinema.

Bad, bad, bad specimens of journalism and um, humanity. Humanity, huge, huge, huge word to be brought up even *en passant* about such roaches.

Kutty soft-lands the 11 a.m. coffee mug on the Bollywood-expert bossman's desk already burdened with more phones and intercoms than you could find in a stock dealer's room. Not many of those red-and-black thingamajigs work. No housekeeper either to clear them from the ditzy desk. Distractedly, Kutty hums on about the local Central Railway Line: it's inefficient... he was 10 minutes late. Upright man this Kutty. Apologises when he should, wanders off towards the canteen with his lunch of three *idli*s and red gunpowder at 1 p.m., does what he is told, doesn't say more than he should. Imtiaz wants to knight him some day or suddenly gift him ₹ 1 lakh to blow up within 24 hours. Startlingly, today Kutty gets into the personal mode, stuttering "Sir, I do admire you."

Oh no, Imtiaz is afraid that this Kutty the Good Man is about to quit. Everyone wants to but is biding time till recession recedes and other media companies renew their annual recruitment policies. With his notepad poised in his right hand as always, the good secretary apologises, "I don't know what to say."

Imtiaz is convinced that Kutty needs a raise but will have to be told firmly that the company's pockets are shrinking. Belts to be tighened for all, money crunch, etc.

The intercom, a functional one, buzzes. Kutty talks into it without talking, and then, in slow-motion looks at his boss. The secretary's eyes ooze concern; his voice drops like mercury, "HR chief...that Delhi bugger...Mishra... *tchah*...wants to see you at 3, Sir."

Bugger? It has happened. Kutty, the militantly loyal Kutty, has lost his cool. Imtiaz's intuition about being fired or quitting from his job is just a lunch soup and salad away. Kutty has blurted out an expletive for the first time within earshot. Dear Kutty announces crisply, "Sir, if you leave, I leave also."

Imtiaz is bemused: both long to leave the jaundiced joint. Why then are Kutty and he flapping about like distraught penguins? He'll leave when he wants to, the ego prods. Imtiaz had launched and laundered the entertainment rag; readers' surveys announced that it was read more than the main "book" (such vaniteeee). He turns red in the face, sweats. His mouth goes dry—dehydration, the kind that strikes before he leaves home for an international flight.

Diplomatically Imtiaz attempts to looks unnerved. Kutty assures him that he'll finish his gunpowder *idli* at the secretary corner itself, not to worry. These people are like that only. Bloody buggers. Imagine they didn't even give him a promotion in his two years here. Chisellers, exploiters. The employer-employee relationship more often than not, in the media sector, unspools towards an unhappy ending. Imtiaz, shut up shut up. Don't let this kill you. That which does not kill us makes you stronger. Quote Friedrich Nietzsche. Not bad that flash of phrase. Maybe he's an itsy-bitsy intellectual after all. "Smile though your heart is aching..." Now that tune was composed by Charlie Chaplin, the lyrics written later and sung by Nat King Cole. Profound pop knowledge...Imtiaz shut your head. Just walk out of Jaundice Zone.

Naah, why give them the opportunity to muck around with your full and final payment, an euphemism for the settling of accounts in a media house.

Coffee quaffed, he waves out to the canteen boy Shanky, as quick on his feet as Mowgli. "*Aaj ka* special *poha*. I'll get?"

No. Imtiaz is nauseous. Although he smiles broadly at Shanky, one of the more cheerful souls in this Dostoevskian establishment of gloom and doom. Quit the negativity Imtiaz, quit just quit, walk over to the *Fundoo* geniuses, the reporters, sub-editors (an extinct race, sigh). Check out the designer's pick of the front page photograph. Must double-check that it has sex appeal: an A-lister heroine's cleavage. Those heroines—*heroines? Mostly decorative props actually*—are everywhere, upgraded by their PRs to vapid cover stories. Asli Maal loves Dhamaka Dude, no it's Funky Funtoosh actually she meets in secret; Pathaka Cheez loves Kiss Machine, no no Pathaki loves Choco Lala who, on outdoor location, loves Phooljhadi who loves...

Shut up, who the hell cares? Er, the nation and the paper's marketing cell. *No Bolly-rubbish, no ads, no revenue, no profit.*

The readers to be catered for are in the age group of 18 to 30. A readership suvey has deduced that the males crave oomph, salivate over girls with raspberry pouts and bare mid-riffs. Female readers buy copies featuring heroes with gym-toned six packs, 16 packs, 60 packs. Oof! Now who's to argue with the marketing team's has-been chief Ravi Rastogi? He could be reminded that cleavages are an old lech's delight? RR would only cough nervously as if he had been caught with his pants down. Quite a case, seriously married, but looks at the office girls through the corner of his eyes. Oh boy, Ravi Ravi Ravi, only human.

Imtiaz is in the midst of the *Fundoo* people. He has to be, so that the chief assistant, a woman with a depressing jute-cotton-mix sweater, Mickey Mouse voice and craters under her eyes, perks up and stops plugging the cricket star, the movie star, the star star, all being managed by her friend, a slithery press agent. As soon as he circles the *Fundoo* desks and chairs, all jammed against one another as in evening traffic, there's a hushhhhhh.

"Here comes the Godzilla who'll kill our copy...that's what you're thinking, right?" Imtiaz says, sending a shiver down the spines of journos, as colourless right now as their computer keyboards. Calcified spines, he's sure.

Of the dozen-strong *Fundoo* gang, there's a brood of reporters and sub-editors who aspire to match up to the standards expected by Imtiaz Ashraf Ali. What to do, what to do?...he makes us cry but that's because he wants us to be better, the best among them are convinced. The faces of the girls and boys, all in their 20s and 30s, are interchangeable. If anyone in the gang has spark, he sees it in Tipu Singh (what a name but it suits him), Jamini Rao (nicknamed Mother Teresa because she nurtures all with her pep talks) and Vidya Nathan (food writer and digesting it).

Imtiaz can smell last night's beer on Tipu. "You had three bottles last night, or four, Tipu? And can you avoid the stinky cigarettes...cheap?" he asks, to evoke a whimper, "Just one boss."

He can tell that they will be late for the 4 p.m. deadline to close the pages. There will be proof-reading errors: the noun *'practice'* will go as *'practise'*; the American *'realize'* will go against the style book's oh-so-British *'realise'*; the articles will go as a string of quotes—he said, she said, Jack and Jill went-up-the-hill prose; Q&As will always start with, "How do you feel right now?" as if the interviewer were a visiting doctor, and they will always end with, "Any regrets?" or "What's next on the anvil?"

ANVIL! "Kill me right now," Imtiaz yells in his head, also wondering if his reporters will describe a 35 mm gauge film as 70 mm. That went out of style with *Lawrence of Arabia, Ryan's Daughter, Mackenna's Gold, Song of Norway*...so what's with you dunderheads?

He can predict that there will be bloomers today. They had made him cry when Guy de Maupassant was spelt as Guyda Mopassa. A rap singer? A foppish fashionista? Never never never mind, he wants to resign anyway three months from now. Dehydration strikes again as his voice cackles, "Baby, but it's going to be today. Toughtoughtough. Handle it."

Hey, no point going through the grammar drill with the *Fundoo* boys and girls right now. He's buzzed. He needs diversion. The Resident Editor, the Front Page

Editor, the Business Editor, the Sports Editor, the Sunday Page Editor, the Saturday Editor, the Metro Editor, the Editor Editor, none of them are around yet. They don't exactly adore him. The antsy Resident Editor has often informed him that there have been complaints against him. Pray what may these complaints be?.. and the Resident Editor looks down at his trousers, Charlie Chaplinesque, halting abruptly at his ankles. "I get phone calls from your Bollywood people every day," Managing Ed rolls his Kathakali-dancer eyes. "They don't like the gossip column. You guys get the lowdown on everyone but we have to be careful."

Help, this greenhorn's probably fallen from heaven.. doesn't have a clue.

Arts Editor rebuffs him with a single line, "Mind your business and I'll mind mine." This goes against the traditional teamwork principle of journalism, Imtiaz knows but alas with this Charlie do as Chaplin does.

The place is crazy. A Senior Assistant Editor subjects the nation to the mental and medical state of her dog Bruno...she writes about her sister's cats supplemented with photos of *Didi* and a litter of kitterns in her terrrace garden. For an X'mas treat, confidences are shared about a cousin's trip around the world. On a sleigh.

Journalism, journalism, come on don't be so prissy, he warns himself. You must have told the nation about your dentist, your doctor, your dermatologist too. Only shades of difference here, so don't go sitting on a high horse. He's done it; he has said it even if it is to himself—*sitting on a high horse*. That shoves his teeth on edge. Hoary clichés like running from pillar to post, at the end of the day, she ticked an invisible speck of dust from her shirt, she has come a long way...his life has been a great journey, nothing succeeds like success...and of late, the jury is still out...*ban them, ban them*.

Newsroom television, on mute, displays a woman in a black business suit, yowling about the Sensex. He looks at a lone tall figure hunched over a laptop—Dinyar Pardiwalla writing away furiously as if his life and the world's depended on it. A ritual. Dinyar invariably unearths some suburban news which the Resident Editor says is not worth publishing: down there in the haphazardly developing suburbs, Malad is to be blessed with another mall; Oshiwara traffic rules are being revised; Dombivli senior citizens are to initiate a *morcha* to protest against the lack of facilities at the Nana-Nani Park. The rebuffed Dinyar pastes these news items on his blog and swears that his reports make an impact.

Imtiaz likes him. At least the guy is committed to his profession much like the snow-haired, about-to-retire Momin Mullaferoze in charge of sifting through the snail-mailed letters to the various editors. Mullaferoze blends into the partitioned desks, eating his silk-smooth *rotis* with onion-potatoes, almost apologetically.

A *roti* roll is offered to Imtiaz; he wolfs it down absent-mindedly. 1.30 now, an hour and a half from that meeting with His Excellency Kewal C Mishra.

Excellency had better not act funny; Arts Editor can act funnier.

The pages for *Fundoo* are moving slower than a fractured snail. He doesn't want to check them today. The errors will send his pressure up. Let them go, let them go. He's been told not to get too "emotionally involved" by the company's CEO aka Bunty *saab,* who never changes his blue silk tie printed with buttercup yellow giraffes. Imtiaz has wanted to yank that tie off, burn it right before the CEO's eyes and gift him a new one.

All is well but Kutty is smiling nervously at him from the secretarial pool. Imtiaz wishes there was a law for adopting senior folk: he'd carry Kutty home, and give him all the peace and comfort he lacks. His son, a shippy, is away permanently, most often in New York. Kutty shouldn't be working anymore. Imtiaz wishes he could break out into that hot-stepper dance for him, *Take it easy policy...take it easy...humma humma.* Hokey song, pokey thought.

Lunch over, it's the time of the day when newspaper staffers trickle in aspiring to snatch strong-meat stories, even if they have to remain within that maze of workstations till the daily is put to bed. They rarely go out on the field, expecting the world to come to them on can-you-hear-me? cell phone lines.

The News Editor arrives, chewing his cuticles as if they were his post-lunch dessert. Imtiaz takes deep breaths...inhale, exhale, breathe from the oesophagus, so said the yoga teacher, demanded and secured ₹ 500 an hour for dispensing such knowledge. If he gets out of there, Arts Editor wants to go coolio—power yoga, jog, read, find a steady girlfriend for steadier sex every weekend.

So *Mr* Imtiaz Ashraf Ali, he asks his voice amplified inside him, go, walk out. His Excellency Kewal C Mishra can go and chase mental volley ball shots. Yes that too. In the company's induction programme, Mishra had screened an amateur AV for the editors, challenging them to lighten up, communicate, *clear* mental road blocks. The AV was packed with excerpts from Bollywood romances. This man had to be nuts. He was, treacle-talking the editors to imagine that they were each holding a volley ball in both their hands. They were then to throw the invisible balls in the air, catch them neatly and throw them at one another. No balls in the net scored. Not for Imtiaz who at the end of the *communications workshop if you please,* had groused, "Nonsense! We're not ten-year-old kids."

Today, he feels like one, at the mercy of the man who had flown down from New Delhi. Imtiaz does a crossword puzzle, browses the internet, chockful of Rishabh Khanna's Marriott exile, but it isn't 3 p.m. yet. Just 2.45 p.m. He gets up from his swivel chair as shaky as the ground under his feet right now, then he sits down. Communication skills demand that he must be fashionably late by 10 to 15 minutes. He makes it five... he's in HR executive Kewal C Mishra's room at 3.05 p.m., smiling goofily and says, "Heyyyy KC, how are you doing? Delhi must be hot, hot, hot."

Kreepola Kewal C Mishra doesn't look up. Busy, *très* busy, scrawling something on paper. "Yes, it's hot," he says, finishes the inking, and looks up dramatically with a blinding smile at Imtiaz. Damn, a canyon cavity. And two missing teeth. Imtiaz wishes to suggest a dental cosmetic surgeon. Doesn't. Let His Excellency look after his own life. And teeth.

The canteen's head steward, yes the *head* steward, shows up to inquire whether the preference for the hour is lemon tea, plain tea, coffee with milk, coffee without sugar, coffee black or...Imtiaz waves him away, "No, no, not now. Later." On noticing a curry stain on the steward's white collar above a black waistcoat, Imtiaz can't resist the crack, "Looks like curry." Head steward nods expressionlessly, "Chicken, Sir." Imtiaz notices that despite his blotchy black-and-white outfit, the man still wears white cotton gloves stained with tea spots. Imtiaz, incorrigible as ever, sighs, "Those spots have been left by Assam tea." Head steward retorts, "All kinds of tea we have, Sir. I'll bring your regular lemon." Not today, not today, maybe later.

Kewal C Mishra watches the editor-steward exchange tolerantly, like a father permitting his querulous children to yakyakayak.

KC's half-cracked smile commands, "Cheese toast." The head steward scampers out to get the Delhi man's working lunch. And now Kewal slumps, his eyes moistening as if he'd just been widowed. Wait, his cellphone shrieks. He answers it, whispering as if he had something to hide, "Not now...yes yes...no...not at all...I'm in an important meeting...yes yes...yes I'll be at that place...Yes yes, I know where it is. At 9...latest 10...*hanh*...all's well...yes see you, see you...I told you 9...or 10."

To convey the importance of the meeting, he jabs the phone on silent mode, and delivers a rehearsed speech which amounts to informing Imtiaz Ashraf Ali that rules are rules are rules in an establishment which prints a family newspaper. So who said anything to the contrary? KC, utterly tragic now, intones that the company stalwartly believes in values, call them old-fashioned but sorry they do believe in values...*and principles.* Imtiaz doesn't know where this is leading; as far as he knows, he is a man of values...and principles...and if he may add, *integrity!* Yahoo, heard of that KC?

The hatchet man isn't reading Imtiaz's face. He is King Lear now, rushing towards a devastating ending—Imtiaz had transferred money to be paid to an American columnist to a girl child's education in Bihar. This indicated embezzlement, fraud. A sum of ₹ 20,000 had gone towards a child's school fees, and not towards the American woman's laundromat bills!

Dehydration hits Imtiaz hard. Is King Lear serious?

The permission for this 'magnanimous' deed had been obtained from the resident COO. Only, the resident COO had quit three months ago. His files had probably been set on fire, so the Arts Editor was being accused of embezzlement. Madly, a Dharmendra scene from *Satyakam* flashes; Imtiaz always believed himself to be *Satyakam 2*. His immediate response—get up, sock this man in the jaw, kick his paunch in, throw water over his dyed hair, tear out his walrus moustache by the roots. Imtiaz was saving the company foreign exchange, initiating a pen pal bond between a girl in Bihar and the columnist in San Francisco, making the world a sweeter place to live in—to be accused of embezzlement.

The stained valet dumps the cheese toast on the table. Lear continues with the drivel he must have delivered every summer, "We appreciate what you have done for the company but we have a certain set of values... and principles."

Values, principles, values, principles, same-same. Imtiaz's eyes are about to fall out from their sockets at the allegation but he gathers his wits and says, "Enough. Do I quit or will you ask me to quit?"

He's given the option of doing it either way. See they are being so forgiving, so employee friendly. Mishra's mouth dribbles cheese. Imtiaz can't help thinking it's the cheapest of cheap cheeses. Unhealthy. This man will die early. Mother Cheese's revenge will be done.

Grandly, Kewal C Mishra offers Imtiaz Ashraf Ali time: Arts Editor can take his time in selecting the day for his departure...three days...four days...a week. Imtiaz says he'll check-out within three minutes, he'll be out of his room with no window, and lousy air-conditioning. KC sighs, "Fine, fine."

There is no need to write a resignation letter. It's already hot and ready; he can smell the cartridge ink. It's in a white envelope, crisply folded, swished open now. And so there it is. Imtiaz signs it with a flourish. Forgive this slob because he knows what he does.

Feeling professionally assaulted, Imtiaz races up to his room, now at a strange temperature, half-freezing, half-sweaty. The lately appointed Managing Editor is sitting there legs folded, his face dark and dingy as if he were attending a wake. He expresses his condolences, swearing that he had no inkling of what the management was doing. Imtiaz itches to tell him, "Buddy, don't pussyfoot with me...you know what's going on...making your guest appearance in my room at the programmed moment."

Managing Editor's open mouth eerily reminds him of a wastepaper basket. He wants to throw a paper clip or two in it but desists. Imtiaz requests the man to just help him get his money and dues cleared. Wastepaper Basket says yes, yes, yes, of course, and exits cowardly. Later, nearly a lakh is creamed off for those wretched flight coupons for trips Imtiaz *did not* undertake for edit meetings, design meetings, launch meetings, re-launch meetings, meeting meetings.

Before leaving, he cradles Tipu's head in his arms. Tipu is crying. Imtiaz had been especially tough on him. Tipu had grumbled that he had been made a punching bag. Okay, one point of view. Another point of view: Imtiaz wanted that bunch with him to rock. Perhaps some of them would.

Ass ass ass, go jump off a cliff with your aims and missions, Imtiaz. Maybe you've just lost the plot, the sub-plots, the whole darn thing.

Normally, he would have shut the door and treated himself to a good, loud, soul-cleansing weep. Soul, ha! The rising temperature in the room prevents that. So he collects his books, artefacts, DVDs, CDs, all that his arm can accommodate.

The receptionist girl, wide-eyed, wonders, "Going so early? Sir, so when is your birthday?" He smiles at her tiredly. And steps out into the 3.30 p.m. sunshine. It hit his eyes.

He can detect the brand of cigarette smoked maybe just ten minutes ago by the taxi driver.

At the zebra crossing, he can guess that the man with muscles bursting forth from the T-shirt is bisexual.

He can predict the next song on the taxi radio, the next advertisement's catchline, the next 15 minutes which will be wasted at the railway station's signal crossing. Always crowded. A truck will discharge gusts of monoxide. He will roll up the window...he knows all this.

He also knows that he is out of Bollywood print journalism. Permanently. There will be no renegotiations, no offers of consultancy, no random freelancing, no summons for a guest column for the year-end edition. *His loss entirely.* Thoughts and words can be hired cheaper by the kilo. A decade or more ago, he had seen an editor, a thinker and doer, shrivel away on being prematurely retired, bitter and resentful. Imtiaz Ashraf Ali, he warned himself, don't become like that. You're better off without *The National Focus Fundoo.* Or are you deluding yourself? Where do you go to from here, my dear chap? To loneliness at the rented apartment in Lokhandwala.

The taxi halts at the traffic lights, inches forwards, predictably hitting yet another snarl of cars, trucks, vans, autorickshaws. The late afternoon sun devours the glistening heart of the day. Imtiaz is already staring at calendars whose months will linger with maddening slowness, whose endless days will imprison him. He's sweating now, doesn't want to, and will not. Cannot. He replays the resignation letter scene over and over again in his head, filing every detail, even inconsequential ones like Kewal C Mishra talking into the phone, informing the caller at the other end that he's in an important meeting, and that he would be at the "place at 9 p.m....or 10..." Hang on hang on dude, incriminating evidence that.

Arts Editor can sniff a lead...the caller at the other end of the line...now who could that be? Kewal's mistress?

A boyfriend? It couldn't be Kewal's wife at Greater Kailash II, New Delhi, she was petrified of the oaf; Kewal's another Rishabh Khanna, isn't he? He couldn't be using hotel rooms though, the stingy bugger. He could never check in at the Marriott like Rishabh Khanna. The hotel doesn't offer *The National Focus* staffers, even the senior ones, discounts...but hang on. Remember, remember, rembember...

Immediately, he asks the taxi driver to return to *The National Focus* office. Cabby reverses gear. They're caught in that railway station traffic jam all over again. They inch...centimetre...they reach the office. Imtiaz has stopped sweating; he's cool, flying higher than a kite with the anticipation of reprisal.

The Rishabh Khanna-at-the-Marriott tittle had been missed by Tipu Singh but three or four months ago, he had burnt Imtiaz's ears with tattle on His Excellency KC. "You're kidding, Tipu," the Arts Editor had blushed. "It's a pity we can't use it in any which way. Maybe if we had an in-house newsletter."

Imtiaz walks right into the cabin of Kewal C Mishra who looks at him expressionlessly. Imtiaz's six-foot frame hovers over him; he imagines himself as a vulture, alighting for the kill. Drawing in his feathers, Imtiaz sits, "KC, we were talking of values and principles of a family newspaper."

"Yes we were...would you like to extend your departure date from the office?"

"No, I have just come to remind you of a certain address...K5 A Silver Springs Apartment, Juhu, Bombay... Mumbai...the place...you must reach there at 9, latest 10 today."

The hatchet man's pen stops scratching in the margins of official documents. After clearing his throat, like a singer before a concert, he says, "I can definitely request Delhi to reconsider your case..."

"Be specific KC."

"You need not resign."

"Really?"

"Let's tear the letter up...you know we are friends. I was just carrying out orders...but I can make a presentation to the board..." Silence and then, "Sorry."

"I didn't hear that...say it again."

" I am sorry...My Mrs and I are breaking up anyway... the person is just someone I have known for some time."

Kewal C Sharma opens a file and hands the resignation letter back to Imtiaz, "There's no need for this."

Imtiaz doesn't accept the letter, "That stays."

This time on his way out, Imtiaz shakes Tipu Singh's hand, "Thank you. You gave me the scoop of a lifetime."

"Which one?"

"You will never know."

CYBERSEX AND THE CITY

A lot can't happen over coffee. At a bookstore café, an assignation between a tall athletic man who crouches to avoid the designer wooden ceiling and a salt-and-pepper, elegant professor, matches the sultry Mumbai October weather. Despite the frosty air-conditioning, they're sweaty, shifty, scanning the menu as if the frayed-plastic single sheet were a questionnaire. They go for the house blend coffee which looks and tastes like warmed-over cola.

The athletic one is a businessman—in hosiery—married, father to teenaged sons who study in an expensive school across the bay separating the city from the suburbs. "I am bisexual," he boasts, "but I don't do anal with guys."

The college professor of Literature, is relieved, "Same here. It's good old-fashioned sex for me. I am still in love with my wife. We have been separated since four and half years. She and my kids are in London with my in-laws. Good to meet you. Is Anil your real name?" It isn't.

Anil Juicy is his sex website's *nom de plume*. He was born Narendra Shyam Singh. Love2loveu, the professor, is Liaqat Sarwar Khan. Businessman is 36, professor 48. Juicy's ancestry can be traced to Rajasthan, Love2loveu's to Lahore; his grandparents had crossed over to Saharanpur and then to Mumbai where they prospered to occupy the upper middle-class berth.

Professor Liaqat doesn't touch the coin-sized cookies on the saucer. Businessman Narendra pops them in the mouth, like pills; ingests them soundlessly. The professor approves of the mouth ballet. This man's no boor; he's let's say 'decent', sufficient potential for a long-term relationship. At the adjoining table, a pretty woman on her second espresso, probably an ad account executive, is tapping away at a laptop. The café's a haven for free wi-fi professionals and business lunches. The men express a faint interest in her. The professor leers, "She's hot." The businessman comes to the point, "So what do you like?" Unlike other netizens the professor has encountered, his coffee mate doesn't add, "dear" or "in bed."

The laptop woman could be eavesdropping, Liaqat cautions Narendra, "Can we come to the details later? Let's just be friends."

"Absolutely."

Like other netizens, the businessman doesn't demand, "Fun first, then friendship." The professor, who has sneaked a look at the laptop screen, re-guesstimates. The woman's probably an investment banker: the lap-page is an organised chaos of numerals and digits.

The man-to-man conversation is proceeding smoothly but slowly. It's likely to end with the customary, "Keep in touch. Take care." If Narendra meant business, by now he would have tapped Liaqat's shoe with his, moved it around his socks, read his face for a "Yes" or "No" but that footsie formula was taking an eon. The professor, never the one to make the first move, used the traditional fast forward, "It's stuffy in here. Let's go for a walk."

Narendra fussed about paying for the coffee, "This one's on me. We can go halves in the future."

Liaqat was encouraged. Narendra was nudging their date further. The investment banker banged her laptop shut, re-opened it, banged it violently, groused to her café neighbours, "Sorry, it's misbehaving." Liaqat checked out the computer's brand, "I have a similar one. Let it cool for ten minutes. It'll be fine." The woman agreed, "Really! These damn things...thank you." Liaqat shuffled out of the café's cluttered table arrangement, "Have a good day Miss...bye now, take care." The probable investment banker perked up, "You too, Sir. Take care."

"Need someone to take care of me, Miss," Liaqat flirted.

"How sweet is that. And it's Mrs," the woman smiled coquettishly before refocusing on the laptop.

Out on the street, the weather was clammy. Heading towards a municipal park, the men maintained a distance. If one's hand brushed against the other's, an apology was tendered instinctively. Neither could give the other the impression that he was desperate for body contact. No meditated touches or words were exchanged till Narendra asked peevishly, "You were turned on by that woman, weren't you?"

Liaqat was pleased; this man was on track. "No, no, not at all," he caught Narendra's hand while crossing a traffic-snarled junction but sought a window in the imminent relationship. "I do like women. The trouble is that they get too clingy, demand commitment, and worse, they're high-maintenance. As it is I'm going out of my mind paying alimony and my children's education fees."

"Alimony must be tough. But tell me, I get this feeling that you would rather be in the company of that woman than with me. Be honest."

"I'd rather be with you...really. I am always honest," Liaqat crowed.

They were playing sexual roulette; such declarations of honesty in website dates were as fickle as a throw of dice. Win or lose, an addictive game was on. They had both played the web route for two years or more, leapfrogging from a quickie to a quickier. Both hadn't received or given love, warmth, sincerity. It was all about a tame or wild encounter in an empty apartment, if not a cheap hotel room which was risky. Police raids couldn't be ruled out. Worse, the partner could have engineered a set-up. A hidden video camera could film the act; blackmail could follow; clips could go viral on the net. Have to be careful—Liaqat and Narendra were in that first flush of mutual distrust.

On a squat cement block serving as a bench, they looked depressed, as if at a funeral. The high-rises encircling the moon crater of a park, cast a gloomy shadow. It was turning darker, late afternoon segueing to evening. Liaqat checked his wrist watch. Narendra felt he was about to be given a brush-off, "Are you in a hurry? Do you have to go somewhere?"

"No, not at all," Liaqat had all the time in the world. "I'm good."

"Good," Narendra echoed. "My wife and kids are away for Diwali, no one at home."

"You didn't go with them?"

"Too much work here. It's peak season," Narendra explained. "Have to go to the factory, check the orders, I am the youngest of three brothers but I do all the running around. Wish I could give it all up. Today I just managed to get away for a few hours. Office has been calling but I've put my cell on silent...for you."

Right. Liaqat had heard this *ad nauseam,* a slogger carrying the burden of a joint family on his shoulders. Equally, Narendra had encountered live-alone singletons, romanticising their loneliness. Predictably Liaqat had said, "I got into this website stuff out of curiosity...to explore my alternate sexuality. Maybe I'm like that, maybe I'm not." This to underscore his 'bi-curious' status on the site. Narendra shifted closer to Liaqat—their thighs made contact—remaining there. Neither registered the touch. Three or four joggers wearing proud Olympics-bound-some-day faces, children exerting their little lungs, a beady-eyed old man with a rosary...not much of a crowd in the park today. Way too dark there, heaps of cut stones, dying plants and balding green patches.

The evening wasn't getting anywhere. Liaqat debated whether to wind up the meeting but didn't want to offend Narendra. So he was relieved when Narendra said, "Okay, I will take your leave."

"Okay," Liaqat jumped up to leave. "Let's stay in touch."

"Yes, let's remain friends."

"Yes. Sex is not everything. But can I ask you something?" Liaqat used the standard punchline. "Are you physically attracted to me?"

"No, not really."

Liaqat was offended. Churlishly, he ended the meeting, "That makes two of us. Delete my number please. I'll do the same."

"As you wish," said Narendra.

"Son of a bitch, if you weren't attracted, why the fuck didn't you say so at the café?" Liaqat flared up, then walked away briskly. He could be easily offended.

A couple of extra-strong single malts downed, he logged on to a website after dinner. "As you wish," the loser had said. What does a wish have to do with all of this? Perhaps because there is no alternative...a very big perhaps.

Another sterile evening. Someone else would surely find Professor Liaqat Sarwar Khan physically desirable. Two messages awaited him on one of the two sites he would check on waking up and before sleeping. One said, "Hi. Interested?" The other said, "Hiiiiii." The more enthusiastic one-word message was from a call boy,

₹ 3,000 an hour. Both messages were deleted. No more Narendras would be entertained. Liaqat had a peripheral agenda: he was connecting with website strangers who could inspire 5,000 words if not more for his collection of short stories. This wasn't a hidden agenda at all. The search for a male muse was stated on his profile, "Looking for someone who can talk about what he has gone through, pleasant or unpleasant." Profession: Writer. Age: 45 (better than 48), educated, lonely.

No picture on the profile stamp which meant that he wouldn't be flooded with responses. Strident requests were made for a clear face picture which he ignored. Routinely, he was messaged for ASL—Age: Sex: Location. For a year, he had met variations of Narendra claiming dissatisfaction with life. In Narendra's case, it seemed that there were increasingly aggravating issues with his joint family. His wife was busy with the daily grind. No stress there. He made love to her twice a week; she didn't suspect that he was bisexual or homosexual by preference. And of course, their children were adorable, absolute treasures.

Most married netizens were giddily happy on this count. Cell phones were kept far away from the wife; sms'es from web pals were deleted.

Bachelors lived with their saintly mothers. Fathers were either not worth discussing or dead. A lean percentage of the younger men responding to the Love2loveu profile, would point out that they were 'straight acting' and 'discreet.' An overwhelming number was proud to be gay, ticking Liaqat off for cowering in the closet. If he was uncomfortable with his sexuality, he was a jerk. Get a life.

Some sort of life he did lead, closeted in his minimalist Juhu studio apartment, substantially stocked with books, DVDs and an eclectic music collection to divert his sense of isolation. Sorry but there are no substitutes for...wait, there could be. Writing about his search for a buddy, a confessional, could be a therapy. He wasn't searching for a fuck buddy. No no no, he was on the lookout for someone he could care for, and someone who would care for him. Care would mean daily phone calls, shirtless embraces, never-ending kisses, trips to a nearby holiday spot. Sex would be a part of the friendship, not its reason.

Profiles of net cruisers required elaboration on the point of smoking. A few admitted they smoked 'socially', whatever that meant. The more daring ones stipulated that they smoked all the time. Many were ambiguous since they were 'quitting'. There was more openness about drinking—'socially', 'all-the-time' and 'love it'. In the domain of turn-ons, moustaches were a must for some; extra-hairy men warned that they were 'bears'; obese ones specified that they had a 'belly.' Height, weight, complexion, in sum the nets were a report on the current state of men. A majority was gym sculpted from 'decent backgrounds'; uncertain ones said that they were 'average'. Pseudonyms were Westernised: Bohemian.rap, Prickasso, Andywarholic, Rouge69, Pisaz, Elton_jani, Depp4U. Indigenous: Kamasutra.king, Chamkachamela,

Bharatnatyamesque, Mughlaidish. Amusing: Dionysus_dance, Pensieve Marxist, Lemon Zeus.

Liaqat's website travels were restricted to online area Mumbai and surrounding cities. No quick trips to the rest of the world. Germany, he considered but it would have been futile. He had tired of foreign jaunts. Too tiring, too expensive, no cattle class compromises. In any case, the immediate aim was to interview Indian men for a short story, question them about their orientation and its consequences if any. If there was mutual attraction, he didn't rule out intimacy-slash-'soft sex'. As a cherubic kid of ten, he had been kissed and fondled by a cousin. A friend had kissed him tongue-to-tongue on sharing a school vacation bed in Mahableshwar, not to forget the locker room shower with two friends after a football match. They had compared each other's organ size—he was inordinately well hung for his height. A gym coach, at school, while handling him on Roman rings, had rested his hands on his testicles, "Nice headlights you have."

Girls at school didn't go for Liaqat Sarwar Khan with the passion he had thought they would. He was 'cute' not 'handsome', excelled at studies, wasn't bad at sports, and belonged to a *nawabi* family. Liaqat dated Doris Sopher, Nandita Shivdasani, Shashi Deshmukh, Dilshad what-was-her-surname? He took them to the movies, discotheques, invited them to his Malabar Hill villa to meet his parents for tea and sandwiches. Gentle manners were exchanged. The girls were mildly interested for a while, breaking up to hitch up with the bad boys who went beyond hugs and kisses. They were more dangerous; Liaqat was sweet, safe. Not quite in keeping with the swinging 1960s. When Nandita had fished out a joint from her clutch, he had refused the offer, "I'm not into drugs." When she lit up anyway, he preached, "It stinks, it's horrible. You'll get addicted." Liaqat was as square as the school's quadrangle.

At college, Liaqat was brainy, aloof. Tentatively, he asked Zarine Shaikh, the daughter of the city's fire chief, out for coffee. She liked him: he wasn't flighty. Boyishly attractive, he topped the class every quarterly term. She borrowed his notes, and was charmed by the chocolate bars, love notes and a brass *taweez* he gifted her. Other girls had oohed over such gifts too, but would have preferred gold chains, perfumes, anything that wasn't cheapjack. The fellow's family was loaded, so why the baubles and beads?

They hadn't kept track. The family's real estate business had floundered. The Sarwar Khans had relocated in Ajmer, sublet their *serai* there to be used as a guest house for visitors to the Hazrat Moinuddin Chishti *durgah*. Liaqat would be sent a monthly allowance. He lived with a widowed maternal aunt at a downbeat address, a rented two-roomer just a yard or two away from Kennedy Bridge where the courtesans were diminishing because of lack of lordly patronage. Old world *tehzeeb* and *adab* had shifted to the courtesan-with-the-heart-of-gold movies. Lucknow was barren of *kotha*s. Mumbai's *kothewalli*s lacking patrons—*qadardan*s they would call the regulars—were reduced to freelancing at beer bars.

While at college, Liaqat Sarwar Khan had watched the women with whirling skirts dance the night away to thunderous *tabla* beats. Quite generously, Kennedy Bridge had offered a ringside view to the open-door *mehfil*s. He didn't venture into the *kotha*s though. He would then have to come up with reasons to explain his fascination for women who sold their terpsichorean femininity. He was attracted kiddishly to film heroines but to Zarine, he was monogamous, perfect. Dull but a darling.

Zarine married Liaqat. At a *biryani-kheer* reception, one of their college friends elbowed Liaqat, "Today's the big night, boss. Lose your virginity...at last."

A staid marriage, a daughter, migration to the UK—in that order. Meanwhile, Zarine's parents migrated to Canada to be with their other daughter and son-in-law. Liaqat's parents were buried within a year of each other, in Ajmer. Life couldn't have been more clockwork in a rented Hounslow apartment, till the birth of their second child. The delivery was complicated; Zarine was never the same again. She was diagnosed as clinically frigid.

The marriage came apart. She moved with the kids to Canada. Her mother wept, "Child, you always have a home in our hearts." Liaqat continued to script news broadcasts for the Asian news channel of BBC as long as he could hang in there. Cost-cutting and staff retrenchment on, Liaqat wasn't needed either by his family or his employers. He applied for a lecturer's position to his old college run by benign Christian missionaries. In five years he earned his stripes—Professor of English Literature, Head of Department. For close to a decade, he felt no desire. No dirty old man urges to repress for the variety of girls in the classroom. Some of them undressed him with their eyes but he could be wrong. A year-long affair with the independent-minded, acne-scarred Inductive Logic lecturer was loveless. A no-strings-attached pact had been agreed upon before they had arrived, in different taxis, to her friend's isolated farmhouse on the outskirts of Pune. Months of passionate trysts later, she broke the pact—marriage or buzz off, Professor, "Stop using me as your sex object." Logic justified.

Chauvinistically, Liaqat summed up his life—he wasn't in a midlife crisis but he wasn't far either. His conversations with women were perfunctory. Poor guy, he loves his wife and kids, he can't do without them. He was pitied. He was drawn to them, sublimated his libido or so he consoled himself. He wasn't turbulent; he was stoic when a family friend from Lucknow visited the city. Shaukat Shaan Haque, in knee-length *kurta,* turned heads. Silken-haired, brandy-eyed with inflamed red lips and easy body language, Shaukat was comfortable with his homosexuality, and wound his hand around Liaqat's shoulder at a restaurant. Liaqat inched away from his guest primly. What if such familiarity was noticed?

Shaukat was staying overnight. From the guest room, he said, "Good night...I'll make it a memorable night for us, Liaqat," walked up to him, kissed him tenderly, licked his earlobes and whispered conspiratorially, "We're alone...alone...just you and I. Fuck the rest of the world. It's beautiful, this moment. What are you afraid of? It's normal." Another kiss, Shaukat pulled him into his arms, "Let me hold you...in my arms."

Liaqat cried. He had ached to feel another body against his; he didn't feign resistance. For that one night, he fell deeply in love with a man, but on waking, was confused, "Thank you, Shaukat but I'm straight. Please don't try that with me ever again. I'm normal."

Shaukat wasn't exasperated. He kissed Liaqat, "My dearest, dearest. Let yourself go. You'll find someone who's worthy of you, and you're worthy of him," and listed the names of three gay websites. "If you don't put your picture there, it'll take time but take my word, you need a friend. I can read that in your eyes."

Liaqat was manoeuvred gently into a parting embrace. Shaukat kissed Liaqat's closed eyes, "What wonderful eyelashes you have. I don't want to leave you. Love you."

"Love? Do you even know what love is?"

Shaukat touched his eyes, "Some day you will see. I didn't say *I* love you. *I* didn't say...*I* have never loved anyone else in my life. Saying love you isn't the same thing."

"Shaukat, if that's what you think, fine. I don't."

"Let me try a test on you. Say *'Love you'*."

"Love you."

"Now say, '*I* love you...like *I* have never loved anyone else in my life'."

"Forget it."

"Exactly."

Just a few hours ago, suspended in time, the room tilting, Liaqat had felt love. He had never been happier, not with his wife Zarine, not with anyone else. He wanted Shaukat to give him that moment again...and again... shut up shut up. Unguarded moment; shouldn't happen ever again. Never never never. Like that school vacation kiss, the locker room showers...come on you're normal, normal, normal. What is *normal?*

As months advanced, Liaqat Sarwar Khan's photoless profiles on two websites attracted a few but regular messages. His self-description of a lonely mature man attracted date-hunters across the board, though primarily men in their 20s messaged that they longed for a father figure, or more brazenly a sugar daddy. 'Looking for a friend' were the candidates he selected for coffee meetings, a standard procedure for cybersex hook-ups. The downright graphic and kinky, masseurs and call boys were deleted. This was entertainment, cybersex charades which enticed time-consuming chats and webcam peep shows. Again and again, any vestige of guilt was erased with Liaqat reassuring himself that the cyber dates would add up to a short story. Who knows, a novel perhaps? On surfing he had logged into a New York cybersex magazine. Its essays and short stories were excellently written and edited. It was also pornographic but then he relished porn. Every man on this planet did. In London he had noticed the Soho peep-joints crammed with tourists. In Mumbai couples sat kissing on the Worli Sea Face balustrade, defying scorching summers and monsoon downpours. Shit shit shit, websites are just another take on lonely hearts' clubs, aren't they?

Liaqat would enter a note on his date on his laptop. The file was titled, 'Cyber People', in case anyone hacked into his comp. Descriptions of the men he met and their chemistry or the lack of it, were jotted safely, self-censoriously. There's too much hacking. Someone could be watching every tap on every computer. If Zarine and his kids ever got to know about his double life, he wouldn't know what he would do. Commit suicide, or shrug it off, "What's it to you? I'm gay and I'm not ashamed of it." The second I-care-a-fuck option was difficult, difficult, impossible. Hey don't go over the top. Not yet, not ever.

Scrolling through the list of his two-year counters, Liaqat was amazed. He had met 30 men for coffee and with half of them he had 'taken it further'. No more than gropes and grunts, certainly not beyond a cold water shower. "You're too uptight," one of the partners had observed correctly, never to message him again. Of the 30, three he rated as 'good friends'. They chatted on mail, recounting their angst at the workplaces where their immediate superiors subjected them to humiliation and piffling salary increments.

Of the loyal website chat friends, Pranay Gupte came out tops for him, dropping by for a glass of wine and updating him on his brand-new boyfriend. Cybersexuals, from his experience, the professor learnt had one *grand amour* in their lives. On losing that Mr Right, Pranay had hopped through relationships although he had become asexual. He could never forget his partner from New Delhi who had jilted him for an expatriate. The partner had left Pranay crying on their New Year's Eve trip to Bangkok. He had bonded on 31st night with an Australian who worked in a multi-national company. Pranay felt deceived, rejected, insulted. Yet, he would fib that the snake was a thing of the past. At long last he had found someone, an ad executive. He'd go ecstatic about the new Mr Right. "He has a great body, a great sense of humour... what more can I want?" He fantasised over another splash of Shiraz at Liaqat's apartment. Liaqat didn't want to hurt him, "That's wonderful," but couldn't stop himself from saying, "I hope he doesn't exist only in your head."

"Talk to him," Pranay jabbed at his cell phone, looked vacantly at Liaqat and sighed, "He's not taking the call. Must be in a meeting."

Liaqat was grateful to Pranay, an undemanding friend who drove a car and didn't ever suggest splitting the petrol tab. He approved of his friend's bravado: the 30-something had adventurously kicked up a cushy job with Deutsche Bank to work for a book publishing firm. "I'm earning less but reading much more. Most of the manuscripts are lousy except a couple of them which are bound to be bestsellers," the friend had recalculated his career.

Soon after Liaqat and Pranay had 'dated' via website, they had ruled out sex. Pranay's heart was still in Bangkok; he was erectile dysfunctional. No matter, he would experience love and sex simultaneously some day. He also knew that Liaqat longed to write his great big novel, pecked him on the cheek one evening, "Prof, I have an offer for you. I talked to my boss...he knows about you vaguely. You guys met up at some seminar or something. We'd be more than delighted if you wrote a novel for us."

A novel's daunting. Oddly an image of mountain-climbing would rush through the professor's mind. Years of research, years of write and rewrites, corrections, intervention from the publishers, who knows what else. Liaqat was flattered but said he wasn't up to it. Novel no, short stories, perhaps.

"Short stories don't sell," Pranay halted. "Still, I'll discuss this with my boss. A limited edition of 2,000 copies could be managed. Now just tell me the sort of stories you'll do."

"Sort of?"

"Prof, you're a sweetie but so inflexible. Just give me an example."

"I'll write about you...my dearest cybersex friend."

"Keep me out of it. But that's not a bad idea...you could do one of the stories on cybersex."

"Or the lack of sex."

"Sweetie, you can be such a baby," Pranay cooed "Just live with it."

Liaqat kissed Pranay, wouldn't let go of him, stroked his neck, withdrew, "This is to say thank you."

"As long as it's only that," Pranay laughed right back. "You know I'm committed."

"In your head."

"Head! Now now, don't get dirty, Prof. Wait, you want to talk to him? I'll call him."

"And he'll be in a meeting."

"Bitch," Pranay simpered. "Gotta go baby. Now you get cracking on those stories."

"As you wish."

"I hate guys saying that," Pranay recoiled.

"Alright, dear."

"*Dear!* Desist! Can't stand that word either. I'm out of here. I'll send you a contract for the book in a couple of days."

"You know I can't stand the word, 'Prof'."

"Picky picky, *dear,*" Pranay bolted, imagining that he was late for a hot date.

Liaqat would ease up with Pranay. He was in a comfort zone with some of his students too, who would update him on their little love stories. An unorthodox teacher, he displayed a radical disrespect for the prescribed text books. He recommended abstruse literature, cinema and music for which the students thanked him profusely. His wards secured top ranks in the board examinations. The college staff—many of them Catholic priests—saw in him a companionable and secular go-getter. Off working hours, Liaqat surfed intensely, hankered after website dates and wrote letters to his children which he didn't mail. His apartment was served by a part-time cook, a maid who cleaned up in the mornings. She was careful about dusting the piles of books—they had to be rearranged just as they were. All quite hunky dory, except that he could not reconnect with Zarine. She was going through psycho-therapy; her parents paid for it. Mother- and father-in-law kept a distance from Liaqat, at most snail-mailing him polite Eid and birthday cards. They could have suggested a reunion with the kids in Toronto. They didn't. It would be awkward; let impressionable kids be.

Remarriage was out of question. The double life on the websites was amusing at the outset till it became a daily fix. The book offer was about to fade. Liaqat hadn't even started writing it. And that token advance? Would the publishers please write it off as a bad debt?

No one knew about the book but Pranay and Liaqat. He wouldn't be quizzed by the whole world, "So, when's your great book coming out? We *so* want to read it."

❧

About the dispiriting meeting with Narendra, he wrote in his unstructured diary:

Juicy2 and Love2loveu were not compatible. Coffee was a waste of time and money...whoever paid for it. The laptop woman, what a fuss he made about her. Love2loveu could have gone for her if she wasn't so young. All the wonderful women in this city are half his age or they're hiding under a rock. Still there was something about that Naren fellow. He was lying but who doesn't? So does Love2loveu. All the time. That's part of protocol. Naren was interesting; I could have got a story out of him. That would have been exploitative but then who isn't? What the fuck is this who isn't, who isn't*? Just admit it, Prof Liaqat Sarwar Khan, you're exploiting other people's lives, you're out to extract your pound of pleasure from someone else's pain. Admit it. You needn't have met Narendra... bloodygoodlookingdude...you could have stopped net-dating after that meeting with Cupid Couple. Such warm, mild-mannered guys they were. You thought they had agreed to talk for the story till they messaged, "We are not ready to make our love known to the world. Hope you* understand." If they had agreed to be interviewed, they would have been my story. The publisher would have loved it, Pranay too. His erectile dysfunction would have been cured, ha ha.

Cupid Couple—Kiran, the 50-year-old airline steward and the retired pilot Patrick, so perfect in their 18th floor apartment, festooned with prints of Japanese calligraphy and a bar of duty-free liqueurs. That's love, so pure, so understated, but I did get shocked. Those lewd men-to-men Kama Sutra poses embossed on their shower glass-pane. That was so crass, so unlike the so classy Kiran-Patrick.

Now Liaqat, why are you bringing them up? You'd forgotten them, except when you're offered almond liqueur. Maybe it's that Naren you have to write about, expiate. Naren on the park bench, wearing his family-made hosiery vest and underpants under a pair of jeans and lime green T-shirt. Not for you, very incompatible.

Judgements come to you easily, don't they? Prof, you're not such hot stuff yourself. Naren was a better person, shy, unaffected. You shouldn't have walked off snootily, not done. So what do you want to do now? Message him, meet him? Forget it. You have never done that. And you won't. He won't respond to your message. Maybe he has already deleted your ID. Let me see, let me see. You won't like it if he has. If he hasn't, he should have. You have to be discreet, you know that. When those fucking coffee dates don't work, the ID should be deleted. Law of the *land, law of cybersex. You're babbling chum. Sum up: Naren, average guy, not suitable, no story, move on.*

Liaqat never revised his entries. He logged off, slept, woke up restlessly close to dawn, logged in. Anil Juicy2 was online. Liaqat messaged, "What are you doing up so late?"

Anil Juicy typed, "None of your business."

Liaqat used the detestable words, "As you wish."

Anil Juicy logged off. Liaqat listened to Bach at low volume, fell asleep, woke up late. No matter, it was a Sunday, the day for his head massage, a beer, a nap. He checked his cell phone; his heart jumped. Narendra had messaged a *non sequitur*: "Today at mall with family."

Liaqat promptly messaged back, "Enjoy, Naren. See you sometime." No commitment made, let him take the first step.

Six months later, Narendra messaged, "Sir, cannot 4get u. Today 7 p.m. Same coffee shop?" Liaqat's heart was thumping; his other encounters hadn't yet yielded a story. When he asked a friend, a film scriptwriter, "Do you see any potential in this at all?" she had suggested a thriller.

What if Professor Liaqat's photo is uploaded on a sex site without his knowledge? He would be disgraced. The college priests would coerce him to resign; his in-laws would gloat; his kids would stop making weekend calls. "The story could be a highly respected man's effort to prove that he wasn't on the prowl for gay bedmates. Someone does him wrong," went the suggestion.

"I don't think so," the professor was tetchy. He couldn't tell the scriptwriter it was his story. Instead, he argued, "That would so trite, banal. That would never happen in real life."

"But who says stories have to be about real life? Use your imagination, Prof."

The cybersex research had been buried without ceremony. Liaqat wrapped up his afternoon class early.

He would end all the nonsense today. He had to. No more website hook-ups, no more uncomfortable encounters, no more no mores but he did want to see Naren again.

Liaqat and Narendra met at 7 p.m. The café was almost empty. They didn't bring up the date gone wrong. Instead, they talked about their children, their jobs, the weather—global warming!—traffic and inflation.

Narendra had shaved, worn musk cologne and a shirt with cufflinks. Liaqat had trimmed his moustache, brushed his hair for five minutes before the parting was right, and put on his linen jacket. Both men had taken care to look appealing to the other.

Naren slid his hand across the café's table to hold Liaqat's, "Sir, if you don't mind, may I say something?"

"Not here, let's go over to the park."

Besides the usual suspects at the park, were housewives, senior citizens out for a constitutional and a persistent tea vendor. Ignoring the *chaiwalla's* sales pitch, the two men occupied a cement block bench.

Narendra moved his thigh towards Liaqat and started, "If you will allow me to, I want to say something... very honestly."

"Of course Naren, go ahead."

"I don't want to be hurt again, Sir. I felt bad when you walked away from me that day...here. You didn't look back..."

"I understand Naren, I felt bad too...but what do you expect from me?"

"Nothing. Sir, I just want you to hold me in your arms. That's all."

"Naren, it never ends there and you know that."

"Yes. I don't know why but...I need someone in my life, someone mature."

"Naren. Frankly I can be very childish, I can't kill the child inside me. I am willing to be your friend, that's all."

"Fine, Sir. Thank you and I do want to say this, Sir.

"None of that love you...stuff please."

"No, it's something else."

"I love you like I have never loved anyone else in my life."

"It's very easy to say such things Naren."

"No it isn't."

Right there in the park at that very moment, businessman Narendra Shyam Singh shuffled closer to Professor Liaqat Sarwar Khan, cupped his face in both his hands, moved his lips on the professor's gently and...then firmly. It didn't matter who saw them or what they said. They kissed deep and long.

A story had just ended. Or begun.

Also Available

The Kept Woman and Other Stories (978-93-80069-27-2)
Kamala Das

"I feel a woman is most attractive when she surrenders to her man. She is incomplete without a man," averred Kamala Das shortly before her death in May, 2009. *The Kept Woman and Other Stories* explores the man-woman relationship in all its dimensions. Deprived, depraved, mysterious, mystical and exalted, each character culled from experience and observation, is an incisive study of love, lust and longing.

The last collection of writings that Kamala Das compiled herself before her death, *The Kept Woman and Other Stories* is a moving and compelling read.

Short Stories * Paperback * 192 pages * ₹ 195

The Company RED (978-93-80070-21-6)
Shantanu Dhar
Soon a major motion picture

A frightful and thought-provoking tale of hunts, The Company RED is the first novel of the RED trilogy by Shantanu Dhar.

A truly contemporary thriller! A must-read!
—Anil Kapoor

Fiction/Thriller * Paperback * 192 pages * ₹ 195

Three Sisters (978-93-80070-55-1) **Man Asian Literary Award, 2010**
Bi Feiyu
From the petty treachery of the village to the slogans of the Cultural Revolution and the harried pace of city life, three sisters strive to change the course of their destinies in a China that does not truly belong to them.

Yumi, the eldest, struggles to retain dignity as her ideal marriage falters. Yuxiu relies on her talent for seduction. And, Yuyang, the youngest, lays her hope in her own intelligence, securing the education that her sisters were denied.

A breathtaking and moving account of the challenges facing women in Communist China.

Fiction * Paperback * 310 pages * ₹ 295

The Eye of the Gods, 2012: An Awakening of the Conscience (978-93-80070-58-2)
Grazietta Salcedo D'Crescenzo
According to the Mayan calendar, 2012 is the year when humanity will witness great changes. These changes, it has been assumed, will be catastrophic but Mayan sources speak of a transition that will take place to a more spiritual way of being. *The Eye of the Gods, 2012:* An Awakening of the Conscience is a first-person account of Ah Ak'tun, born to Mayan parents in the Mayan region of Tikal, Mexico in AD 673. After the death of his father he is adopted by a venerable high priest who nurtures him to be his successor and weans him in the ways of the ancient Mayas and their special relationship with nature. He teaches him the significance of belonging to a priestly class that is duty-bound to oversee the activities of governors, merchants and politicians during times of war and peace. Ah Ak'tun in turn recounts his tale, giving us special insight into the cosmology of an ancient people.

Fiction * Paperback * 375 pages * ₹ 250

Cry of the Giraffe (978-93-80069-48-7)
Judie Oron
Labelled outcastes by their Ethiopian neighbours because of their Jewish faith,13-year-old Wuditu and her family make the arduous trek on foot to Sudan in the hope of being transported to Yerusalem and its promise of a better life. Instead, they are herded into a squalid refugee camp until the day soldiers round up Wuditu and scores of others, forcing them back to the Ethiopian border.

Throughout her harrowing trek across the scorching sand, and the humiliation, fear and despair she later faces as a slave, Wuditu's only hope is to be reunited with her family in Yerusalem.

Based on real events, this story mirrors the experience of thousands of Ethiopian Jews who fled from hatred, persecution and brutality to a new life in their spiritual homeland.
Fiction * Paperback * 232 pages * ₹ 195

Thunder Over Kandahar (978-93-80069-47-0)
Sharon E. McKay
Best friends Tamanna and Yasmine cannot believe their good fortune when a school is set up in their Afghan village; however, their dreams for the future are shattered when the Taliban burn down the school and threaten the teacher and students with death.

As Tamanna is faced with the prospect of an arranged marriage to an older man, and the Taliban target Yasmine's Western-educated family, the girls realise they must flee. Travelling through perilous mountain passes, the two unaccompanied teens find themselves in mortal danger as they confront land mines, a suicide bomber, and roving bands of the Taliban. But when the two girls are separated, they are left without the one thing that has helped them survive—each other.
Fiction * Paperback * 288 pages * ₹ 195

FORTHCOMING TITLES

Faction (978-93-81607-13-8)
Khalid Mohamed
This is a brilliant collection of untold stories from a by-invitation-only set of Bollywood film personalities. A surprise packet.
Fiction * Hardback * 250 pages

Delhi OMG! (978-93-80070-68-1)
Vinod Nair
Delhi OMG! traces the journey of Dinesh, a middle-class offspring as he meanders through life and the city of Dilli in his struggle for survival. **Fiction * Paperback * 312 pages**

Newsroom Live (978-93-80069-30-2)
Prabhat Shunglu
In an era of corporate journalism, the media industry is willing to experiment with the irrational and the perverse. *Newsroom Live* attempts to capture the shenanigans of the newsroom and its illicit relationship with power corridors and corporate sharks.
Fiction * Paperback * 250 pages

Short Stories from Modern India (978-93-81607-16-9)
Edited by Suresh Kohli
This brilliant collection of short stories from some of the finest literary voices across India explores themes as diverse as the aftermath of Independence, industrialisation, nation-building, corruption, and more, compelling us to ponder over the universality of literary themes.
Fiction * Paperback * 300 pages